# The Corpus
# in the Library

# Irish Fiction Published by Dalkey Archive Press

Alf Mac Lochlainn

# The Corpus
# in the Library

stories and novellas

Dalkey Archive Press

© 1996 Alf Mac Lochlainn
First Edition

    Library of Congress Cataloging-in-Publication Data
Mac Lochlainn, Alf, 1926-
    The corpus in the library : stories and novellas / Alf Mac
Lochlainn
      p.   cm.
    I. Title.
PR6063.A25317C67    1995    823'.914—dc20    94-8746
ISBN 1-56478-068-6


Dalkey Archive Press
Illinois State University
Campus Box 4241
Normal, IL 61790-4241

*Printed on permanent/durable acid-free paper and bound in the
United States of America.*

# Contents

# The Corpus in the Library

Out where imagination arches
Chilly points of light transact
The business of the border marches
Of the Real, and I—a fact
That may be countered or may not—
Find their privacy complete.

—THOMAS KINSELLA

# Preface

S ome of the people mentioned in the following pages are real, for example Horst Ernestus and Thomas Aquinas. The statement that my wife disapproves of the way I hang shirts in wardrobes is false, as false as a statement in an earlier work that she considers my spare-time literary activities a complete waste of time. Although she did none of the typing, I am grateful to her for much else. Grateful, too, to Dr. Joan Byrne, who developed the performance-enhancing 'Dame,' which is also false.

A. MAC L.

**sárú,** *vbl. noun, masc.* Violation. **s. cóipchirt,** infringement of copyright. **s. mná,** rape of woman.

**bean,** *fem. (gen. sing. & nom. pl.* **mná,** *gen. pl.* **ban)** Woman.

It would be nice and dramatic if I could say that I woke up on the morning after learning of my father's mysterious death and faced with terror the thought of dressing myself. Unfortunately it wasn't a bit like that. The morning of which I write was a fair while after my father's death and was so ordinary that I am not sure I am really recounting the events of a single morning or perhaps conflating bits and pieces of several mornings, and of course I am sure to be ignoring miscellaneous forgotten scratchings and stretchings and the regular matutinal pee and minor ablutions, regularly inserted at the vest/underpants stage. The deepest probing of my subconscious could hardly find any real terror and would find it difficult to assign any role in the whole proceeding to my father's life and death, mysterious though any coroner would have to find the latter. My meetings with my father for anything more than 'Good morning' and 'Good night' had been infrequent until his last years but always quite cordial and he had, I suppose, contributed something to whatever intellectual equipment I possessed.

To get back to the dressing, though. Terror is certainly too strong a word for my feelings but disquiet there was because I was faced as ever with a lifelong problem to which I had never found an adequate solution. Which garment should I put on first? At my time of life I had few ethical principles left more complex than the rules of the road but some situations do call for a grand theoretical framework from which a local and specific rule of conduct may be derived. One such grand design is the Newtonian postulate: apples fall. Since in my pelt I am of fairly consistent weight per foot of height (I have a small backside), it behoves me not to upset vertical equilibrium by injudicious addition of garment-weight here and there indiscriminately. Clearly if I were a medieval knight or a deep-sea diver and began my dressing by putting on a massive helmet I would fall flat on the floor. An extreme case, granted, but it does illustrate the need for care. So what should I do first? Sit up. Fold back the blankets. Swing the legs out and place the feet on the floor in one easy, graceful movement. The feet were obviously going to be very important. My friend Horst Ernestus, otherwise an estimable character—tolerant, witty, intelligent, and fortunately bilingual—suffers from one defect which may yet prove dangerous. It is his practice to begin dressing by putting on his socks. His wife says he looks silly but that is not the point, for just as a heavy helmet causes top-heaviness, so socked feet will cause top-lightness, however slight, and a tendency for the top to drift forward, ahead of the sock-heavy feet, when the body is in forward motion. So whatever should go on first it shouldn't be socks if forward movement is contemplated. Balance is the whole secret.

Balance requires regular and even imposition of weight above and below the centre of gravity, that is to say above or below the waist, give or take a few inches. A perfectly straightforward intellectual problem, then, and a reasonable approach to the solution and not a flutter to be seen of any subconscious father-fixation.

My father, as indicated, was not exactly a major influence in my life, but he did leave me a quantity of papers after his mysterious death in the Reference Room of Rathmines Public Library. Among them were the uncorrected galley-proofs of an auctioneer's catalogue.

## Papers of a Scholar and Other Properties

We are under the owner's instructions to dispose of the papers of Charles W. Morgan[1] and the following choice lots will be offered for sale by auction at our rooms on Tuesday the 11th of October commencing at 11 a.m. . . .

5. Theatre playbills . . .

16. *Wer ist wer,* 1934, heavily annotated by C. W. Morgan. The annotations apparently represent Morgan's projected corrections toward later editions . . .

28. Letters of W. H. Bowker, publishers, to C. W. Morgan, 1928-49. These letters are mainly requests for and acknowledgements of contributions to bibliographic and other reference works. Included are some drafts or copies of letters by Morgan to the publisher, often querulous in tone: ' . . . and if you think I can go on churning out this stuff at the same rate while you go on paying for it at the same rate you must never have heard of inflation. My note on Sir Owen Hyshins contains a large number of new "facts" . . .'

37. Drafts by C. W. Morgan in ms. or typescript with extensive annotations and revisions of entries for (unnamed) reference works. The entries relate to persons and institutions, including schools, colleges, clubs, political parties, etc., and range from the fragmentary ('Served with the Irish League of Nations troops in Eritrea!!! A risky one?') to the elaborate ('Judge of the Appellate Division of the Irish Central Court. B. 1895 Claremorris, ed. C.B.S. Claremorris, U.C.Lim. and Law Soc, bar 1924, inner bar 1931. Chmn. Comm. on Legal Costs, 1934-42, lect. admin. leg. prac. R.U.Belf. 1935-39. Councillor Internat. Comm. on Jurisp. M. 1938 Emer McGovern, 1s., 1d. Club: United Grads., Royal Lanesborough Y. (commodore 1940). Res. Ardmore, Eaton Sq., Dub.').

My only systematic reading on the subject of dress had been Mecredy and Stoney's penetrating essay in *The Art and Pastime of Cycling* (Dublin: Mecredy &

---

[1]Charles W. Morgan was not my father's real name.

Kyle, n.d., c. 1889).[2] This essay bears all the marks of careful and thorough research and the facts are presented with admirable clarity. The work is marred by only two faults: the treatment of trousers is so cursory and dismissive (the authors are invincible in their determination to promote knee-breeches or knickerbockers) that no mention whatever is made of bicycle clips, and there is throughout an impassioned advocacy of the theories of Dr. Jaeger concerning the noxious exhalations of the body, its 'self-poisons' as he so quaintly termed them. Jaeger, it will be remembered, was the originator of the 'wool next to the skin' thesis.[3]

---

[2]This is a real book.

[3]I can give here only a summary of the Jaeger thesis as presented by Mecredy and Stoney. 'Fluids, and solid bodies which are porous,' they say, 'possess the faculty of absorbing gases under cold, and giving them out again under warmth, and when a solid has absorbed gases, an additional means to expel a portion of these is by wetting it. We may take it as a general principle that health is fragrance, disease stench, and hence those solids which absorb evil gases are to be avoided as articles of clothing. They are earth, charcoal, wood, and all proceeds of the vegetable kingdom, such as linen, cotton, jute, etc.' (It seems safe to condemn garments of earth, charcoal, and wood. Wooden shoes have had some vogue in rural Holland and elsewhere but earth and charcoal have never been popular as raw materials in the rag trade.) 'Fragrant odours are attracted from the air by all animal fibres constituted of horny substance, as wool, hair, feathers, horn, hoofs, and white or tanned leather. . . . So far so good' (they say—far, yes; good, I take liberty to doubt). 'Certain materials absorb evil gases, and certain materials absorb healthful gases, in both cases liable to be given off when subject to warmth or wetting. Now, the body gives off certain exhalations, which may be distinguished by the terms "salutary" and "noxious," and which may often be perceived by the organ of smell. If one is in a cheerful, pleasant mood, and in good health, the scent will be agreeable and the exhalations salutary; but if sorrowful, depressed, in pain, or unwell, the scent will be disagreeable and the exhalations "noxious." . . . The odour of the woolen material . . . is salutary, attracting the blood to the skin, which becomes warm, and enables the moisture to evaporate more speedily. Dr. Jaeger thus sums up on the point: "If we employ materials for our clothing,

The thing to do clearly was to organise a deft and rapid switch of pyjama pants for socks[4] before standing up and I managed this without much difficulty. Before standing up I had also to sketch out my future plan of action: vest for pyjama jacket (sitting)—but this would leave a cold and immodest midships section. Down the next snake. I took off the socks and put on underpants,[5] cursing them yet again as they caused me

---

bedding, and furniture, which, in a cold and dry condition, lay hold of our self-poison—i.e., of the mal-odorous portions of the body's exhalations—and when warm and moist, give it out again into the atmosphere, we are the defenceless victims of all variations of temperature and humidity; we have to deal with a foe which is at times concealed, but only to gather strength in the interval to attack us afresh." . . . To guard against these dangers, wool, and wool alone, must be used, and a few illustrations will show very forcibly the vital importance of avoiding all vegetable fibre as clothing. Suppose . . . a man sits with starched shirt-front bending over his desk, the shirt-front stands off from his body, becomes colder, and fills with noxious exhaled vapours. When he rises and straightens himself the pressure of the shirt-front against the warm body causes the surplus exhalation absorbed to rise, so that there is a concentrated re-inhalation, while the woolen shirt-front would allow the noxious vapours to get away into the air.'

"STOCKINGS: These should be of wool and not too heavy. Tight garters are most injurious. They impede the circulation, and may even cause varicose veins, and this is especially the case if the garter is secured above the knee. The best plan is to garter very loosely *below* the knee with a strap, and then turn the top of the stocking down over the garter, and then button or strap the knee-breeches or knickerbockers a little below the garter. . . . Suspenders are used by some, and many still use the ordinary elastic garter, but if used it should be broad and loose. It is a good plan to soap the heel and toe of the stockings, as this prevents the foot from getting sore' (Mecredy and Stoney, *op. cit.*).

[5]'DRAWERS: If possible these should be dispensed with, but in the case of many it will be found necessary to wear such during winter. They should be of very light woolen stockinet. . . . The Jaeger combination of shirt (or chemise) and drawers, in one piece, is a very convenient garment for cycling, as nothing can get out of place' (Mecredy and Stoney, *op. cit.*, in an unusual piece of candour, if not downright coarseness).

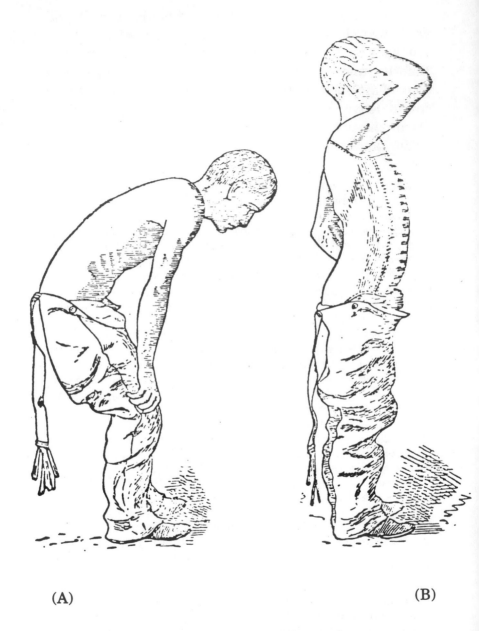

(A)                                                        (B)

The author (A) ponders over the braces problem and considers his next move and (B) realises that donning the Jaeger vest while ignoring the braces may be fraught with danger.

unmentionable discomfort. I had long since concluded that they are produced under an ancient and exclusive franchise granted by the Guild of Merchaunt Taylours, in some secluded convent by ladies in religion with little experience of the world. I took off the pyjama top and managed to reach my vest, haul it over, and slip it on. Now I could at least stand up and I did so with a small feeling of triumph.

I was for many years a regular patron, one of very few regular patrons, of the Reference Room of Rathmines Public Library. It was an oblong, high-ceilinged apartment, with shelves on all walls, even surrounding the window which gave a view of the town hall and fire station. The shelves were filled with dictionaries, concordances, gazetteers, compendia, multivolume sets of lives of the saints, Bibles in various languages, encyclopaedias, directories. Occasionally I did history and geography exercises there which had been assigned in school, or Latin translations spoilt by uncouth use of dictionaries more complex than I could handle, or English essays, larded with obscure and ill-understood quotations culled from yet another unwieldy tome.

We were taught by earnest young students aspiring to the priesthood and their lessons in history and literature were a little too heavily laced with allusions to ideas first adumbrated by learned fathers of the early church. The name Aquinas recurred and I determined to go one better by finding out what he had really said. The Reference Room of Rathmines Public Library did not let me down but I was considerably taken aback to find that what he had said, all eleven volumes of it, was in Latin, and in a Latin very different from that in which Caesar, having drawn up his cohorts in battle array on the third day, ordered the cavalry to advance on the left wing as quickly as possible so that the enemy might not escape. There was one large single-volume job purporting to be *The Layman's Concise Guide to the Great Philosophers* but it lacked its earlier pages and began with the closing paragraphs of an essay on a man apparently called Averroës, followed by Bacon and Berkeley. They were all intensely interesting but of no use to a sixteen-year-old smart aleck trying to outsmart student Thomists at their own game.

My father's career, which must remain one of the curiosities of literature, had begun in that very room many years before when a genial and learned librarian, Mr. Heaney, had warned him against accepting as fact everything that appears in a reference book. Publishers of these books, Mr. Heaney explained, deliberately include misstatements. Such misstatements are included in the reference books in the interest of copyright protection. There is no copyright in facts. If I happen to discover that the summit of Mount Everest is 29,001 feet above sea level and publish this fact, I have no claim on anyone who repeats it. Worse again, if I spend a lot of money accumulating the information I put in my *Personalities of Irish Life* I have no redress if some buccaneer extracts all the facts on sports stars, rephrases them, and publishes them as *Who's Who in Irish Sport.* While one could make a claim that one's 'b. 2.4.1916, m. 2.5.1937, 2s.' is creative writing, it would be hard to make it stick. If, however, one creates, invents, an entirely new personality, the entry describing him or her, however dense and abbreviated the style, is undeniably a piece of literature, as imaginative as six hundred and odd pages of a fictional day in the life of a fictional advertising canvasser looking for a son to replace a dead baby and a father dead by his own hand. *And* as fully entitled to copyright protection. So your pirate is in real trouble if he pinches your 'Kachaskach Khan, runner-up l.-w. wrestling,

Tailteann Games, 1924, b. Mongolia,' or your 'Hamstrung (Bent), Norway, winner of international marathon, Tailteann Games, 1928.'

It occurs to me that herein may lie the explanation for the occurrence in a biographical dictionary of contemporary poets[6] of a strange entry describing my friend Rudi Holzapfel.[7] The entry, which has always puzzled me, reads in part as follows:

> Holzapfel, Rudi (Rudolf Patrick Holzapfel). Pseudonyms: Rooan Hurkey; R. Patrick Ward. Born in Paris, 11th December, 1938. Educated at Los Prietos and Santa Barbara Catholic High Schools, California; Artane Boys School, Dublin; and Trinity College, Dublin, B.D., 1961, M.A., 1964.
>
> Married to Clara Mangan; has three children. 'Traveled to the Near East in 1965, joined Al Fatah (Arab guerilla movement) and tried to establish Irish-Arab Freedom Party; lost membership in Irish Republican Army following denunciation of its communist sympathies; joined Orange Order, 1968.' Teacher of geography at St. Phillip's School, Burley-in-Wharfedale, Yorkshire, England, 1967. Since 1962, Deacon at Our Lady Queen of Peace Church, Dublin. Since 1968, teacher of bibliography, Bradford Technical School, Yorkshire. Address: c/o Department of Italian, University College, Galway, Ireland. . . . For a valuable study of his work, Mr. Holzapfel suggests J. P. Dargan's *Rudi Holzapfel, the All-American Arab* (Dublin: Allan Figgis, 1968).[8]

'I admit,' my father said, 'that I lack the perseverance and monomania of your genuine novelist but I have enough imagination and verbal skill to see me through the short run. I had a simple letterhead printed announcing myself, under an assumed name of course, as a literary agent and circularised a large number of publishers of reference works. I included a simple specimen of the work of an author for whom I presented myself as agent—I just invented a place,

---

[6]This is a real book.
[7]This is a real name.
[8]This is not a real book.

more or less at random, a kind of typical Irish rural place-name, and wrote a description of it in the manner of a nineteenth-century gazetteer. And would you believe I got a commission. Look, here it is.' He took down a fat red volume from the shelves of the Reference Room of Rathmines Public Library, fingered through it, and pointed out the entry for Sir Robert Acton. 'I was asked to provide what the publisher coyly called a protective entry for *A Dictionary of the Titled Classes*, and there it is, my first publication in a genre which I can claim to have invented, the ultra-short story, shorter than short.'

He sat back with some pride as I glanced over the potted biography of Sir Robert. 'A bit short on plot,' I hazarded. 'Plot!' he exclaimed and followed it with the sound I recognised as the one conventionally written 'pah.' 'Plot! Sure plot is only just another device for putting things in order, like the alphabet. A to Z is as good any day, all you have to show is that your string of statements starts in one place and goes through certain others on the way to the end. It's not plot poor Sir Robert needs, it's body. It's purely a formal aesthetic consideration of course, in practicalities it doesn't matter a damn since nobody's ever going to look him up anyway. Come to think of it, they'd better kill him off, he's getting a bit long in the tooth and some prying idiot of a journalist might dig him out as the last of the class of 1911 or something. Might be a few bob in that.' He scribbled a note on a scrap of paper. 'Anyway I needn't have worried about the lack of body, sheer pressure of work began to give them all classmates and fellow soldiers or whatever was needed.'

ACTON, Tagoat, co. Wex. Sir Robert A., 6th bt., succ. his uncle Sir Mortimer A., 5th bt., 1922. Ed. Burlington, Osgood Mil. Acad., Sub-Lt. 1911. C.I.M.E. 1917. Ret. 1919. Club: Molesworth (Dub.). Res. Tagoat, co Wex. (Ire.).

I could now move about the room in comparative safety and was free to consider my next move. Pants up, shirt down, socks up, pullover down, shoes up, jacket down, all seemed fair enough. But are socks and shoes singular or plural and is a jacket not around rather than down? Hardly much danger there, I felt, as the jacket undoubtedly hangs from the shoulders and therefore is definitely a downward item. The case of the waistcoat,[9] if I was wearing one, was less clear. Its tightness around the torso and the flimsy nature of the material in its shoulders suggest that it adheres by friction rather than gravity.

The only indubitably 'around' item is the belt and this is beyond question in a safe, neutral, and balanced equatorial zone. A minor matter is sometimes raised, that of direction. A good case can be made for wearing two belts, one with the free end passing from the left through the buckle, the other with the free end passing from the right, thus avoiding a tendency to turn left or right which either alone might impart.

> AHERNE (Most Rev. Dr. Patk.) M.A., D.D., S.T.C. Bp. of Raharney and Conary, Apos. Del. Kilrockan. Ed. St. Nathi's Dioc. Sem., Dunboyne Univ. (B.A. 1927, M.A. 1928). Ord. Pentecost 1929. C.C. Templenee 1929-32. Prof. St. Nathi's 1933-34, Pres. 1935. Admin. Rathbeggan 1940-43. Sec. dioc. comm. educ. 1937-43. Chairman National Commission of Enquiry into Technical Education 1941-43. Dom. Prel. 1941. Succ. late Dr. Cathal Gurney as bp. and apos. del. 1944. Patron West Regional Bd. G.A.A., Connacht Coursing Club. Res. Aras Nathi, Rathbeggan.
> —Clergy of Ireland (McGill, Duffy & Nolan, 1947)

---

[9]'WAISTCOAT: This garment should be cut high, and lined with very light flannel. When riding in warm weather it is better not to wear one, as even when it is of the most porous material it confines the exhalation of the body to some extent' (Mecredy and Stoney, *op. cit.*).

Shoes plus socks equals either two or four, depending on how you look at it; shoes plus socks plus old-fashioned sock suspenders, if I could get them, equals three or six. This should leave enough freeboard to accommodate even a shirt with separate collar,[10] tie, and even a hat,[11] as well as standard items such as collar-attached shirt and jacket; the optional bicycle clips in reserve below should deal with any unexpected developments aloft.

My father waxed reflective and nostalgic sometimes about his early days. 'It was hard work, I can tell you, and damn little thanks I got and damn little reward, grinding out the stuff week after week, never the satisfaction of any acclaim or acknowledgement half the time, or with the American publishers anyway, when I never saw the books and never even knew if the stuff was used. And it was only paid for like a miserable penny-a-liner, so you can see I had to be pretty economical. That's what solved part of my problem, actually; if I had already created a decent public school for the Anglo-Irish gentry to send their sons to why should

> CODDINGTON, e. and b. (I), cr. 22.2.1801 (e.) 23.4.1664 (b.) Godfrey 5th e., 14th b., b. 16.6.1904 Bloomington, Salop. Ed. Glastonbury. Gaz. 2 lt. 4 D.G. 1.1.1924. A.D.C. Viceroy of India 1926-31. Res. Coddington Hall, Kilnahee.
> —Living Irish Peers (Figgen Allis, 1938)

---

[10]'COLLAR: Linen collars should not be worn when cycling—in summer at all events. Woolen ones may be procured, or else an all-wool cricket shirt, with collar, may be used. It is often well to carry a woolen comforter, which should be immediately put on in case of a sudden dismount in cold weather' (Mecredy and Stoney, op. cit.).

[11]'HEADGEAR: It should be light, well ventilated, porous, and of animal fibre, and should contain no leather lining. . . . The helmet, though peculiar-looking, is most satisfactory, especially in hot weather. . . . Whatever is worn, see that all leather, cotton, and even silk lining is eliminated, and that only animal wool is used for this purpose' (Mecredy and Stoney, op. cit.).

I waste time and effort on creating another one for a clergyman of the established church to be head-master of? And Burlington, I had decided, was quite high church. You'd be surprised how many of its old boys did well in the church, and in the army and the diplomatic too, not to mention the Indian Civil. And obviously it soon became too elaborate for me to rely on memory and I developed a neat card index of my

> CORDIGAN (Jeffrey), (Diarmuid Ó Cardagáin), Senator. Chmn. Western Contractors Ltd., dir. Genug Lock Co., Western Engineering and Construction Ltd., Moy Joinery Co., Cement Supplies Ltd. B. 1.4.1888, Kilnahee. Ed. St. Nathi's N.S. Lieut. C Coy., 2nd Western Brigade, I.R.A. 1920-23. Memb. Rathbeggan U.D.C. since 1926, chmn. 1932-38. T.D. 1936-39. Sen. 1940-45. M. 1919 Sinéad Aherne, 1s., 1d. Res. Sarooban, Kilnahee, Rathbeggan.
> —Irish Business Leaders (I. N. Agency, 1946)

creations, all classified, religion, politics, and public life, scientists, technicians, artists, writers, places, movements, my own abbreviations, my own degrees and honours, public bodies, the lot.'

I ventured a question: 'But wasn't there always the danger that you'd invent something that existed already?' 'Of course, my boy, of course, and why do you think I spend most of my working life here in this Reference Room of Rathmines Public Library? If half of these books'—he waved an arm about and then the tattered copy of *The Chemist's Laboratory Companion* (edition of 1908) caught his eye—'well half of their modern counterparts have stuff by me in them, the rest is stuff I've had to avoid.'

> 'DAME' a novel phenylethyl ether: chemistry and biological activity. (Order no. 762206.) Oheictigearn, Donal. D.Ph. UCLim., 1933. Supervisor Prof. Pfitzinger.
> The work of Piness and associates (1930), Alles (1931), and Prinzmetal and Blomberg (1932) drew attention to the usefulness of the amphetamine drugs in medicine. The work reported in this

*thesis was undertaken in an effort to produce a compound with enhanced activity but without the toxicity of the original compound.*

*Coupling of dl-α-methyl-α-hydroxyl-phenethylamine with dl-α-methyl-α-bromophenyl-ethylamine using the Pfau-Pfitzinger-Pforr reaction with an alkaline catalyst under high pressure resulted in a linking of the two amphetamines through an oxygen atom to give the ether bis-αα'-dimethyl-ββ'-diamino phenylethyl ether ('DAME').*

*Biological results in a test system using mice and primates are reported, which show that the compound when administered orally exerts a hitherto unequaled effect on the uptake of oxygen by muscle and exhibits greatly increased activity as a stimulant of the CNS. Unfortunately the aim of finding a less toxic product was not successful and doses only slightly in excess of the biologically effective dose proved fatal.*

—International Guide to Dissertations *(1936)*

I continued to slop and slap barefoot about the bedroom in the cool safety of my vest and underpants, plotting carefully what I might do next. The thing to avoid was sudden change in top or bottom weight at the end of the dressing routine and of each phase of it. I could work up gradually to the real crunch problem of heavy leather shoes versus heavy tweed jacket (the shade of Jaeger applauding at last). Odd shirts and socks and so forth in the meantime shouldn't really count that much. I opened the wardrobe to reach for a shirt but

Structure of the doubled amphetamine molecule

withdrew my arm hastily. The shirts were facing the wrong way.

'Don't be so damn silly,' my wife exclaimed once, 'what difference does it make which way they face?' 'Look,' I explained carefully, 'for our mutual convenience we've divided this wardrobe into a Ladies and a Gents, right? You can hang your blouses and dresses and things any bloody way you like on your side but I like my side to be organised properly. I'm fairly ambidextrous but I do favour my right hand slightly, right? And all our coat hangers are those wire ones that come back from the cleaners, right? So you have to be pretty damn careful that the actual hanging hook goes over the hanging bar along the top of the wardrobe from the outside in or you'll have the divil's own job getting the bloody thing off if the bar is even halfway near to being full, right? So I take the hanger in my right hand, look, with my hand just under the hook, look, and with the hook pointing to the right, see? Then I take the shirt or whatever it is by the back of the neck in my *left* hand and with my right manoeuvre the wings of the hanger into the shoulders, through the front opening, right? So now I have in my right hand a hanger with a shirt on it all ready to go into the wardrobe and when I put it in with my right hand and the hook going over the bar from the outside in THE OPENING OF THE SHIRT HAS GOT TO BE FACING TO THE RIGHT, SEE?' 'All right,' she said, 'keep your hair on, you and your miserable big ends and little ends.'

*HANLEY (Declan J.), 1918-1949. All Collegians will have learnt with deep regret of the death in a riding accident on Oct. 6, 1949, of Declan Hanley. He was one of our most distinguished old boys and a regular attender at Collegians' dinners. An intimate friend writes:*

*Decky, as he was universally known, was a splendid fellow and all his old schoolmates watched him rise to an unrivaled position of*

*power and influence in his chosen way of life with pride and grati-
fication. The stages of his brilliant career are well known but are
worth recalling as a reminder that in this wicked world sterling
qualities do sometimes bring their reward even if the tragedy of
Decky's early death must also serve to remind us that indeed we
know not the day nor the hour when the angel of the Lord will call
us.*

*Decky was marked for success from his earliest youth. He was
one of that happy band of boys in Kilnahee who had the good for-
tune to come under the influence of Fr. 'Packy' Aherne, distinguished Collegian and now Most Rev. Dr. Patrick Aherne, Bishop of
Rabarney and Conary, during his curacy there. Dr. Packy already
represented the best type of modern churchman and, while a
staunch though tolerant conservative in theology, he taught all with
whom he came in contact, in particular 'Fr. Packy's boys' as they
were affectionately known, that the true witness of the layman is in
the world as it is, in commerce, sport, or the professions.*

*Decky was the keenest of the boys, an altar boy, member of the
choir, corner forward in the hurling team, and regular attendant
on Fr. Packy's famous greyhounds. He was the first beneficiary of
the scholarship instituted by Fr. Packy when he became President of
St. Nathi's and his record in scholarship and sport fully justified the
confidence reposed in him. He went on to take his degree in U.C.L.
and only a commitment to a brilliant career on the playing field
prevented his achieving the high academic honours of which we all
know him to be worthy. Decky always said, in his modest way, that
of all his sporting triumphs the one that gave him most pleasure was
the victory of one of Fr. Packy's dogs!*

*On graduation he entered the public service, joining the young
Department of Irish Industry. From his parent department he was
soon seconded to serve as secretary to the National Commission of
Enquiry into Technical Education and it was in this position that he
really showed the talents which were to make for his success when,
within a few years, he took the bold decision to leave the public service and pursue a career in the private sector, becoming succes-
sively secretary to Church Property Management Consultants, Ltd.,
accountant to the Construction Industry Employers' Federation,
and finally Managing Director of Ecclesiastical and Scholastic Con-
tractors, Ltd., a company which he quickly piloted to its present
leading position. He had, of course, a place at the boardroom table
of several other companies and the business life of the country will
miss him sadly.*

*None will miss him more than his sorrowing wife Sinéad (née Cordigan) and young children Jenny, Godfrey, and Patrick. To them the sympathy of all St. Nathi's Collegians will be extended.*
(The Collegian, *annual record of St. Nathi's College, 1950.*)
—Requiescat: Select Irish Obituaries *(Irish Times Pub. Co., 1951)*

My shirts were hanging with the openings facing left. With misplaced kindness, after washing and ironing them, she had been even more helpful by putting them away for me. And one of them was on a hanger with the hook pointing outward. I took the whole lot out (there weren't really that many), rearranged them, and took one at random. While I am very careful about how shirts are hung in wardrobes I don't really care that much which shirt I wear.

I carried the shirt toward the chair where my pants had been dropped overnight, slipped on the shirt,[12] and without moving a step started to put on the pants.[13]

---

[12]"SHIRT: In accordance with the principles just enunciated, this garment should be of pure undyed and unbleached wool. Dyed wool should be avoided, on hygienic grounds, and also because when it has been chemically treated it is more liable to shrink . . . the shirt should be double-breasted, and should button at the shoulder. For use, when cycling, it should barely reach to the hips. The Jaeger shirts are much longer, but by ordering the vests (which are considerably cheaper), and getting button-holes worked in front of collar and utilising them as shirts, a considerable saving may be effected' (Mecredy and Stoney, *op. cit.*).

[13]"TROUSERS: The misguided individual who cycles in trousers suffers in comfort and health. We have long fought against this senseless and unsightly mode of clothing the legs: notwithstanding the power of fashion, we are not without hope that the neat, comfortable, and hygienic costume of the cyclist will cease to excite attention when worn during one's ordinary business or occupation.

'KNEE-BREECHES: Knee-breeches, when well made, are more comfortable and neater than knickerbockers. They should fit closely, but should not be too tight, and great care should be taken that they do not grip the knee at any time when riding. To this end it is better to patronise a tailor who is accustomed to make cycling suits. . . . The waistband should be of woolen material, and in no

*KILNAHEE, par and tnld., bar. of Rathbeggan. Galway 55m. Pop. (1861) 1,117. Early and probably fabulous records state that in this parish was fought a famous battle, the Catnamolg, between the Firbolgs and the Milesians, the latter proving the victors subjugated their defeated opponents to the rank of slaves who were forced to carry stones for building purposes for their conquerors. Some scholars aver that the term 'bolg' which gave its name to the vanquished race can be translated in either of two ways, one which delicacy prohibits us from indicating, the other signifying bag or budget to denote the receptacle in which the building stones were carried. There is a well in the parish to which the peasantry resort in great numbers on the 15th of August annually in the hope of being vouchsafed cures for sore eyes and other ailments and, it is to be regretted, for the consumption of spirituous liquors in large quantities.*

*Much of the surface is under bog, the remainder arable and pasture. There is a small limestone quarry occasionally worked. Goats abound and are the source of the infrequent meat on the table of the common people, amongst the older of whom, especially in the more remote parts of the parish, the ancient Erse dialect is still freely spoken. The only seat of note is Coddington Hall, residence of Lord Coddington, in the rustic gardens of which is a romantic folly locally designated the 'Sarooban.'*

*The living is a rectory impropriate to the Earl of Coddington, a resident and improving landlord. The place of worship is a handsome edifice erected in 1835 with the assistance of the Board of First Fruits. It is in the restored vertical English decorated style and the interior is embellished with edifying memorials to Godfrey, 10th baron Coddington, and his wife Alicia. In the Roman Catholic divisions it is part of the neighbouring parish of Templenee and there is a small chapel in the village of that name.*

—Statistical Gazetteer of Ireland *(Longman, Trench, 1867)*

---

other position is the result of cotton or linen more disastrous. The fit should be close around the hips, and in most cases it will be found quite unnecessary to wear a belt. Braces we are entirely against, as they cause an uncomfortable drag and heat the shoulders. Double seats are generally uncomfortable, and single seats will, perhaps, be found the best. A pocket on the back of the hips is a great convenience' (Mecredy and Stoney, *op. cit.*, with unwonted slyness).

Engraving after academy
portrait of Godfrey, 4th earl
of Coddington ('Gorrai na
mban'), ob. 1907.

Lt. Diarmuid Ó Cardagáin,
O.C., C Coy., 2nd Western
Brigade, I.R.A.

Eventually I plucked up the courage to put a moral point. 'But supposing,' I asked my father, 'some poor eejit picks up one of those books in fifty or a hundred years' time, he'll think it's a real list of the titled people or whatever of the date of publication, won't he?' My father paused a moment and then let go with something he must often have rehearsed to himself. 'Facts, you mean,' he said, 'you mean he's looking for facts. Well take it from me there's no such thing as facts in the abstract or the absolute. There's so many of them and ninety-nine point nine percent of them are so trivial that they make just a finely divided universal sludge that we're floundering around in, a limitless cosmic ocean. Only their occasional mutual support now and then coagulates some of them in a little gobbet of harder stuff here and there. I've invented new theories in astronomy and bacteriology, chemistry, dentistry, eugenics, fractional distillation and gerontology, and so on and so on, I've created archbishops and zoologists, butchers and bakers and candlestick-makers, yachtsmen, xylophonists, and wheelwrights, and they all hang together, they're all as self-consistent as the rest of the other stuff in those books.' And he waved again with dismissive contempt at the shelves of the Reference Room of Rathmines Public Library.

> Mac LOCHLAINN (Alf). Librarian and writer. S. of Chas. W., b. Dublin 1926. Jt. founder and hon. sec. De Selby Soc., chmn. Galway Aerofoil, Boomerang, and Kite Club. Publs. inc. Marx and Spencer: A Critique of Materialistic Sociology (Berkeley: Univ. of Calif. Press, 1951); Out of Focus [a surrealist novella] (Dublin: O'Brien Press, 1977; Elmwood Park, IL: Dalkey Archive Press, 1985).

'We live under a torrent, a spate, a deluging cataract of so-called facts. All the books in the world couldn't and don't begin to recite the millionth fraction of the facts that could be stated, I mean fully and extensively stated, about, say, you and your surroundings when you're just barely beginning to be conscious, say when you open your eyes in the morning when you're waking up—your height, weight, age, colour of hair, colour of eyes, number of teeth, the chemistry of your whole body, your position in the bed, the materials and shape of the bed and bedclothes, the geometry of the room and the disposition of the furniture in it—for God's sake, did you ever see a diagram of a complex organic molecule? And there's billions of them in your little finger and the relationship of any one to any other or all the others is a fact or facts, we can only make feeble attempts to chart the high spots. And my chart is as good as anybody else's. And you haven't even begun to dress yourself.'

MAITH AR N-AIS OLC AR N-ECAN (Lit. Good our goodwill, bad our forcing) If you do it our way so much the better for you, if we have to force you that's your hard luck. Cardingan (Ire.), Cardigham, Cardington, Coddington, Kiddington.
—Your Ancient Family Motto Explained
(New York: McCarthy, Murphy, 1931)

'How they're to be presented of course is another matter entirely, and damn the bit of difference whether they're what you'd call real'—he smiled wryly—'or what you'd call fictitious. The more economical the better. Take a letter, like *m,* million or mile or meter or even man, like in a cast list where you'll read "10m, 5w." Context will always tell you what it means

MORGAN (Chas. W.), historian, biographer. B. Dub. 1888. M., 1s. Hobbies: curling, croquet, caber-tossing, calisthenics, communism, crossword puzzles, catalogues, carpentry, catch-as-catch-can, cameras. Chmn. Collegians Chess Club, Coill-uachtar Cine Club. Pubs.: contribs. to var. wks. of reference; The Layman's Guide to Cetology.

and anyway no letter means anything at all outside of its context. In reference-ese it means "married."

M. 1.1.1940 is perfectly adequate; if you really want a prosy description of a wedding there are hundreds available, folksy provincial newspaper, ritzy society magazine, anything. Saying something about mathematics shows the kind of danger you can avoid by being economical. If I write 2+2=4 nobody feels called upon to preach a sermon on it, but if I write it out in words just as if it was part of a conversation "when you add two and two you get four" some blundering idiot has to jump in and make a big thing about it. "Ah, yes, but," he says, "don't modern theorists say that it depends what direction you're going and what speed and after all someone else speaking of his own experience is quite entitled to say that *for him* two plus two is something quite different." No, my boy, just stick to the plain and simple unadorned statement and never mind those facts.'

*O hEichtighearn (Donal), prof. of vet. biochem., U.C.L. since 1937. B. 1908. Ed. St. Macdara's Coll., S.J., and U.C.L. Sc.B. 1929, Sc.M. 1930. Dir. field trials N.-S. S.-und-A. Fab.-Werk, 1931-33. D.Ph. 1933. Lect. Vet Med. U.C.B. 1934-36. Pub.* Field Trials of a Novel Phenylethyl Ether: The Chemistry and Biological Activity of 'DAME' *(Hanover, 1934).*

—Irish Universities Directory *(1937)*

'But the statement should be true,' I ventured weakly. 'True, true? What is truth? Every definition begs the question. Remember Saint Thomas, even. A proper equalisation of the thing to the mind, that's what he said truth is. Look here.' He fished into an inner pocket and landed a crumpled sheaf of printed papers. 'This is from a standard reference source, I mean a real one, I didn't write any of it. *Adequatio rei intellectu,* there you are. But how do we know there's a

*ST. NATHI'S, dioc. sem., Kiltinagh, pres. An tAth. P. O hEichtighearn. Sec. sch. for boys, prep. for studies for the priesthood, civil service,*

*matriculation. 190 boys, 75 boarders. Fees (tuition) £20 per term, music, French, games (oblig.) extra. Own grnds., rural setting. Train to Kiltinagh Station, 3 mls. Enq. to Rev. Pres.*
—Guide to Catholic Colleges in Ireland *(1937)*

thing out there with a relationship to a mind in here?' Again he waved an arm around, then thumped his forehead with the heel of his hand. 'We know it only with the mind in here, so what I project out there from inside here is as good as anything else any day.'

Legs of pants, and sleeves of anything for that matter, have a physical property which so far as I am aware has never been noted in the scientific literature, even by workers as obviously diligent as Mecredy and Stoney: they are shapeless when empty but when full assume the shape of their contents. They are a form of anti-liquid. While being filled, however, they are expanding straight lines from crotch (armpit) to cuff, as the foot (fist) runs down (along). An inside-out shirt, which I occasionally suffer, can be turned right-side-out by a skilful dresser making use of this property. He can push his fists into the reversed shoulders and affect a progressive topological inversion of the sleeves and hence of the whole garment in one continuous smooth sliding action.

'I wrote an entry for myself once, when something was asked for in a hurry, it was easier than inventing, I changed a few things of course, everybody always changes something when they're writing about themselves, not that they can really write about anything else anyway. And you have to leave out so much that no matter what you write it has only the barest relationship to what people are pleased to call the truth.'

'But somebody reading it can work out more of the truth about you by what you've left out, what you didn't say rather than what you said?' I queried.

'Look, suppose I put in what they work out by what I've left out, there's another layer below that of what is still left out and will they work down to that too? And if I'd put in even that and so on and on and down and down what depths can I leave that some silly mole won't insist on excavating with his ridiculous calculus of infinitesimal differences? So why bother with anything but the top layer? If omission is untruth then one layer is no better or worse than a hundred.'

Sketches of C. W. Morgan's invention, the 'Isograv,' for unifying garments and distributing their weight evenly over the body.

I do not know exactly when my father decided actually to live in the Reference Room of Rathmines Public Library. It was somehow fitting that he should do so, that a man with such a burning passion for coherent untruth should bind himself so finally at the foot of those cliffs of incoherent truth. He smiled a little sadly as he told me of his decision. 'You can tell your mother where you have seen me,' he said. 'It is pointless to attempt concealment of this passion which I cannot master. I think she will understand and know that this is something which I must do.' Bombastic, if you like, but such a long-standing attachment had made this ending inevitable and his preparations were well advanced when he made this heartfelt declaration to me. The mechanism of taking up residence was quite simple and it was my small part in it which frightened me into silence when the coroner was investigating the mysterious circumstances of my father's death. I did not know if a charge of being an unwitting accessory to involuntary suicide would lie and I was after all doing no more than filial piety dictated.

To take up residence in a library is not as difficult as one might think and I do not hesitate to reveal my father's ingenious method, for just as would-be library residents may read this and hope to learn how it's done, so will library custodians read it and learn to take appropriate countermeasures.

The equipment needed was quite cheap and compact: five or six yards of tough webbing as used in upholstery, cut into pre-measured lengths, filled a couple of pockets, no more. Another pocket had plenty of room for the rest of the gear: a small box of thumbtacks, a somewhat larger box of galvanized flat-headed felt nails, an awl, and a small but wide-jawed screw-wrench.

After a meticulous dry run at home, he sat down at the long heavy table in the Reference Room of

Rathmines Public Library, drew from his pocket the end of the first length of webbing, and with careful and privy thumb-work attached it lightly on the inside of the hefty side-timber on which rested the broad leaf of the table. I was sitting opposite and my only service was in my turn to reach down, grab the hanging end of the webbing, and thumbtack it to the inside of the timber on my side of the table. Next move the parent's. A good stab with the awl and further energetic thumbing got one of the felt nails engaged through the webbing into the timber; then the opened jaws of the screwwrench were placed over both the side of the timber and the head of the nail and by being screwed closed squeezed the nail home. This was tedious but discreet as the butt of the wrench sat snugly hidden in my father's lap as he worked. Six slings (twelve ends, thirty-six nails) were not an immense task, over several days, and yielded a safe hammock of considerable weight-bearing capacity.

Traffic of readers in the Reference Room of Rathmines Public Library was always light and my father had no difficulty, on completion of the hammock, in carrying out tests nor in practicing entry and exit routines. Actual use of the residence was less simple and involved careful timing to make going out and coming home coincide with appropriate periods during the library's opening hours. By midmorning, when two or three people had been in and out of the Reference Room, which was under the nominal though remote control of the staff at the main library control desk, who was going to notice one going out who hadn't gone in? And later, in the evening, who was going to notice one less going out than had earlier entered? The only hazard was in picking a time when he was alone in the room for nipping into and particularly out of what he called his 'slings and narrows.'

I was really the only one who suffered any nervous embarrassment, because I was never sure my father wasn't hanging under the table on which I was doing my Latin exercise, a mere two inches perhaps above his nose.

> *SAROOBAN, Rathbeggan, is a substantial modern residence but is of special architectural interest as it incorporates an earlier structure, a typical 19th-century romantic folly. This and a few acres of ground adjoining were acquired on the breakup of the Coddington estates under the Land Acts by the present occupant, Sen. O'Cardigan, who in 1937 added the imposing flat-roofed e. and w. wings faced in local cut stone, and the ornate classical portico of eight fluted Corinthian columns, the pediment embellished with an allegorical figure of Hibernia. The entrance hall consists of the early folly, built in rubble masonry and with its walls now pierced to give access to the spacious wings and at rear to the ballroom, decorated throughout in black and white artificial tiling.*
> —Debrett's Mansions of the United Kingdom,
> *vol. 12*: Eire *(Debrett/Country Folk, 1947)*

I had finally reached the point at which I could equip myself for normal human locomotion in the real world. I could put on my shoes.[14]

The brown pants required the brown shoes and these were happily a four-hole pair which exhibited, ready for tightening, the correct centrally displayed top X. Better minds than mine have been bent to this matter of shoe- and boot-lacing and have failed to provide a

---

[14]"SHOES: Boots should never be worn for cycling. They do not afford free egress to the exhalation of the foot, they interfere with the free action of the ankle, and tend to weaken it by affording an artificial support. This question of covering for the feet is a most important one. The foot perspires freely, and if there is not free egress for its exhalation it becomes hot and sore and gives off an evil odour. Theoretically, woolen shoes should be used, and inconveniences from wet feet would then become a thing of the past. . . . The Jaeger Company manufactures a special kind . . .' (Mecredy and Stoney, *op. cit.*).

satisfactory solution. The earliest Irish investigators gave enduring form to their speculations by carving their experimental designs on the edges of stone slabs. The more remotely academic among them ultimately wasted their energies in the sterile 'art for art's sake' decoration of the great illuminated codices.

Briefly the problem is as follows: to find the lacing pattern which will achieve maximum (i) closage, (ii) distribution of stress over length of lace, and (iii) speed of loosing, combined with minimum (i) redistribution following breakage, and (ii) length of lace. (Solution to be generalised to cover 2, 4, 6, 8 . . . 2n lace-holes.)

Lacing patterns are sometimes further complicated by intrusive twisting of the laces. Few things are more annoying than the spoiling of a nice trim centered top X by uneven twisting. It is seldom worth trying to restore

Early Irish caricature of child in difficulties while being taught how to lace shoes. (After the Book of Kells.)

balance and symmetry by imparting to a crossmember of the X a twist exactly the same as that disfiguring its partner. The effort nearly always fails and time and efficiency are lost through having to go back to the beginning, undo the whole thing, and start again. The twists derive, apparently, from an unevenness in the tension of the individual fibres which are braided to form the lace and could be obviated only by a complete teasing out and re-assembly.

Unfortunately, as it turned out, my consideration of socks and shoes was not concentrated on their number and weight but rather, as indicated on the lacing pattern and further, on the adhesive sock/shoe interface. The sock-sucking shoe is a positive heart-scald. Take a bath, dry the feet carefully, trim the nails, dust the feet and the ankles and the shins with talcum powder, take a clean pair of socks. Even under these conditions, surely the optimum, a shoe or boot with the slightest roughness or furriness on its inner surface can clutch and chuck so resolutely and tenaciously at the sock that after a mere couple of hundred yards of quiet walking the heel of the sock has been dragged forward into a knotted lump under the arch of the foot and the infuriated wearer is lucky to find enough of the ribbed top of the sock protruding above the upper part of the shoe to enable him to TUG THE BLOODY THING BACK UP WHERE IT BELONGS.[15]

---

[15]Mecredy and Stoney had not, apparently, the advantage of using *The Human Foot: Its Form and Structure, Function and Clothing,* by Thomas S. Ellis (London: Churchill, 1889). 'That a long train of evils are more or less attributable to defective foot-clothing,' Ellis writes, 'is beyond all reasonable doubt. But while this may be recognised and admitted as regards boots, few persons at all realise the amount of injury traceable to socks and stockings. . . . The ordinary medium-pointed or even-sided sock is productive, directly and indirectly, of much of the evil put down to the charge of boots, and should be discarded by all who wish to use their feet as feet. . . . The

The end came suddenly in one way and with agonising slowness, I am sure, in another. Neither my father nor I could have known that the Dublin Corporation Waterworks planned a major seek-and-repair operation under the pavement just outside the door of Rathmines Public Library for a long Easter weekend, from the evening of Spy Wednesday until the Wednesday of Easter Week. A huge hole yawned there, watched over by a man beside a brazier, and my father's standard fallback safety device was denied him—the late-night sneak-out via the main door, the spring lock of which could be opened from the inside and would snap into the closed position when pulled to from outside.

I first noticed the obstructions to the door of Rathmines Public Library while on my way to Mass, on Spy Wednesday morning, in the nearby copper-domed parish church and my mental perturbation coloured grievously my appreciation of the Pascal rituals. I could hear only those fragments of the readings which referred to my father's predicament and my own: separation of the father and the son, the splitting of a

---

separate stall for the great toe is an element of great importance, but as regards function there is no advantage in a separate stall for each of the smaller toes. . . . Under some conditions of unhealthy skin it is of decided benefit, but only then. On the material of which the sock is composed the comfort and healthiness of the skin much depends. It is important that it should be of wool not of a character liable to mat together; that it should be porous, readily absorbing perspiration and readily allowing it to evaporate. Cotton does not readily absorb moisture at all, but once wet remains clammy and is a long time drying. As a material for clothing a foot pent up in a boot it is most unsuitable. . . . For the unpleasant character which the perspiration sometimes assumes, readily amenable to judicious treatment, no remedy is efficacious unless there be free exposure to the air. To this end cloth shoes are highly desirable.' Ellis's work is available in summary in Felix Wagner's *A Hand-book of 'Chiropody,' giving the causes and treatment of corns, callosities, bunions, chilblains, and the diseases of the toe-nails, with advice as to taking care of the feet* (London: Osborne, Garrett, 1903).

sacred unity, a self-imposed exile from that unity, and a lonely death. The existence of the separated son was reduced by Friday to a tiny presanctified wafer and on that day he cried to his father, 'Why hast thou forsaken me?' By Sunday, though, there was some reassurance, the son, risen and glorified, had again become one with his father.

My personal idiosyncratic preoccupation too seemed to have become a recurring motif with the inspired authors. Already on Spy Wednesday the Gradual included the ominous phrase 'I stick fast in the mire and there is no sure standing.' The twelfth prophecy on Holy Saturday contained particular detail which could relate only to me. Bad enough, you might think, for Sidrach, Misach, and Abdenago to be bound and cast into the furnace of burning fire, without the added indignity of being so cast 'with their coats and their caps and their shoes and their garments.' Were their persecutors a figure for extremist Jaegerians? Had they discovered that the cap, coats, et cetera, were made of materials of vegetable origin and dealt with them accordingly?

I was pretty frantic when I arrived at Rathmines Public Library on the Thursday morning of Easter Week and even more frantic when I saw that the glass door and wooden wicket into the Reference Room had not been opened. I enquired at the main desk and was told that the Reference Room was being closed as an economy measure to allow for the switching out of a few radiators, even though the main summer switch-off was only a few weeks away! 'Did you want anything special? We can always bring them out here to you.' 'Ah, no, I just usually do my eckers in there.' 'But aren't you still on your Easter holidays?' I blushed furiously (at being caught out as a swot, I hoped they thought) and stammered that there were a couple of things I wanted to look up but it didn't matter.

I stood up after my shoe-tying, slipped on my jacket,[16] and walked toward the door of my bedroom. I must have made some silly mistake in counting, probably in the matter of whether shoes, socks, and similar pairs are to be considered as singular or plural, because after the first pace I sensed a distinct and uncontrollable oscillation in my over-carriage. One step farther and I fell forward flat on my face.

It was naturally some time before my father's remains were discovered. The erosion of his corpse was a reprise of the earlier erosion of his great intellect and was fittingly surrounded by Averroës, Bacon and Berkeley, Condorcet, De Selby and Descartes, and by walls lined with books striving ineffectually to impose order on the chaos of the universe. Much of his flesh had emaciated away before he died in his pitiful bed.

His clothes too had gone and it is not clear why they had been outlasted by the webbing, which survived to perplex the investigators. We cannot be sure that my father was aware of the Jaeger principles. If he was, he clearly did not abide by them. His hammock sling was of woven jute, almost certainly the origin of the sackcloth so frequently referred to in Holy Writ, for example in the tenth prophecy on Holy Saturday, and manifestly a dangerous vegetable fibre. The noxious exhalations of his body must have been pretty ripe toward the end.

---

[16]"THE COAT: The material of the coat should be some porous woven stuff of wool . . . and the very smallest amount of lining and stiffening should be used, and it should be of woolen material. . . . Every shred of cotton, or of linen, should be eliminated. . . . No matter how strictly enjoined to the contrary, tailors are very fond of using cotton for the lining . . . and will even assert that it is utterly impossible to dispense with it. . . . The Jaeger Company prepare a specially woven woolen stuff for the purpose . . .' (Mecredy and Stoney, *op. cit.*).

Eventually the Reference Room of Rathmines Public Library was reopened and a crossword enthusiast was the first reader to slap a heavy dictionary down upon the table. The gristly connective tissue around my father's joints had gone by this time and the thump of the fat volume was followed by the rattle of something hard on the floor. The reader peered under the table

 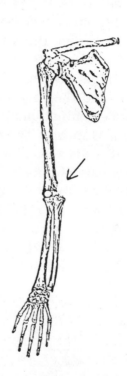

Diagram showing the Maintenance of the Erect Attitude. *Muscles which keep body from falling forward.* 1. calf; 2. thigh; 3. spinal column. *Muscles which keep body from falling backward.* 1. leg; 2. thigh; 3. abdomen; 4. neck. The arrows indicate the direction in which these muscles act.

Simulation of anatomical structure of right arm of C. W. Morgan, demonstrating the absence (arrowed) of the inferior posterior process of the humerus, over which the ulnar nerve would pass in a normal subject.

and so was witness to what ensued. The loss of a thigh-bone, for that is what had fallen, upset the delicate balance of the skeleton and all the heavier bones followed, arms and legs, ribs and skull, and finally a lighter shower of fingers, toes, and bits of the spine. As the prophet Ezekiel had exclaimed on Holy Saturday, 'The Lord set me down in the midst of a plain that was full of bones . . . now they were very many on the face of the plain and they were exceedingly dry. And he said to me, dost thou think these bones shall live?'

The Chief of the Detective Division of the Gárda Siochána, the Chief Medical Officer of Dublin Corporation, and the City Librarian later carried out a thorough examination of the Reference Room of Rathmines Public Library. They found, apart from the main elements of the skeleton, a number of minute crystals of carbonate of lime, identified as otoliths,[17] and a single detached fragment identified as the inferior posterior process of the right humerus of the deceased Charles W. Morgan, who, the coroner determined, had met his death by misadventure in the Reference Room of Rathmines Public Library.

*ZOZIMUS BORGIA. To the studbook he was just 'br. d. 1926, Rev. P. Aherne (Q 889586) by Poison Pen-Ballad Singer,' but he will always be remembered for the glorious ending to his chequered career. His first public appearance was at Newbridge where he won the Belsize Stakes and challenge cup for sixteen no-course maidens. He was very much fancied for the event in the long-odds betting and ran two stylish courses. Then in the semifinal, despite a severe grueling behind a hare which refused to take the escape, he managed to pick up in his stride and win. In the deciding course he led Lonely Mounty a length and legged his game. He had very few successes on the track during a brief stay across the water but older coursers will always say there has been nothing in living memory to compare*

---

[17]Lee is of the opinion that the otoliths and maculae form the organ of statical equilibrium.

*with his performance in the Easter Cup in Thomond Stadium in 1933, where he set a phenomenal record of 27.3 secs. after a bemused break from the trap and a lazy glance around, followed by an electrifying acceleration which took him past all challengers to cross a full ten lengths in front—and drop dead from heart failure thirty seconds later!*

—Irish Greyhound Greats
*(Clonmel: Nationalist and Sporting Press, 1944)*

**Medal struck in commemoration of Zozimus Borgia, 1934**

*Extracts from reviews of the Australian edition of*
*'The Corpus in the Library'*

'He has invented an entirely new genre . . . not a who-done-it, rather a who-done-what.' —*Claremorris Chronicle*

'Reflections on the professional competence of the staff in charge of a well-regarded public library are entirely out of place in a piece of what some may over-generously call comic fiction.' —*Irish Library Journal*

'Deliberate confusion between the author and the main protagonist put an end to any hope that there will be found in this work any elucidation of the Berkeleian problems in the field of cognition.' —*European Annals of Philosophy*

# Present Tense

There are all sorts of reasons why I should wonder about the advertisement, but equally all sorts of reasons why I should consider it perfectly legit. In the first place, nobody gives you $750 for doing almost nothing. Not that it actually says they give you $750 for doing nothing. Participants may earn *up* to $750; perhaps a good deal less is implied. Then again, that's a fair sum of money, presumably tax-free, and specially added to your social security, old age pension, or whatever entitlements you have over the age of sixty-five. And the ad invites applications only from people between the ages of sixty-five and eighty-five—why this prejudice against the aged, I mean the genuinely aged?

'Healthy people (aged 65-85),' it says. Healthy? I resent the vague implication that most people 65-85 aren't healthy, that the unhealthy have to be weeded out. Well, who's completely healthy at sixty-six anyway, or fifty-six, come to that?

There's nothing really wrong with my health. The odd creak in the joints (specially the left knee and base of right thumb), stiffness as I straighten, dizziness if I straighten too quickly when I get out of bed, loss of some power in the caliper action of finger and thumb, and I'll tell you a funny thing, every so often, maybe at monthly intervals or thereabouts, I get an itchy spot on the inside of my right thigh, just above my knee, a real fat bit, and I'm full sure it's one of those valves in a big vein or artery in there, the makings of a varicose vein I suppose but I'm not one to go bothering a doctor for something as occasional as that. So all in all nothing really life-threatening and surely perfectly fit to participate in a Sleep Study (their capitals).

All I have to do first of all is keep a simple sleep journal at home, and that's the next reason for distrusting the ad. If they say something is simple, it almost certainly isn't. When the instructions for the home-assembly rocking-chair kit say 'simply trim the squared ends of the crossbars to fit the holes in the long uprights,' be sure that trimming those square ends is to take a full week's work with your penknife, the blunt plane that's on the floor of the garage behind the push-bike, and the scuffed zero-grade sandpaper you use for brightening the cutlery.

What a simple sleep journal is I do not know. Nothing elaborate, I suppose, just times of retiring, times of waking. Anything else would quickly become less or more than 'simple.' Like dreams, say. I sometimes write down notes of my dreams, the structured ones, that is, not just the bits and pieces of yesterday's non-adventures, so why not get up to $750 (or part thereof) for a sleep journal without dreams? Dreams of course are always in the present tense, like the way unsophisticated people relay the stories of films to their friends: 'There's this guy and he has a gun and he goes up to this bank and he says to this other fella behind the counter. . . .' And genuine journals are written up at the end of a day and are always in the past tense.

Then I just wear a small temperature monitor for one week. Not that bad. I remember a small patch stuck on my arm like a Band-Aid, for testing if I have TB, and another one for the gentle infusion of a nicotine substitute which is supposed to cure the smoking habit (doesn't work), something like those I imagine.

Then there's the legit side. The ad is in a most prestigious journal, the *Harvard Gazette,* no less, of March

27th, 1992. Let's not fool ourselves; it's not as if there is only one Harvard newspaper, there are probably dozens, written by students, dons, administrators, cranks, and left in heaps for free distribution all over the town-within-a-town in Cambridge which is Harvard. I dread to think of the acreage of forest chopped down every week to sustain the Harvard newspapers. Ironically enough, if you search diligently in some far corner of the Yard you will probably find a Harvard-Baumwachsener Institute for the Study of Arboreal Depletion. But even though it's free, the *Gazette* is not one of the cranky ones nor the alternative ones, it's mainstream stuff.

Then that hospital they mention in the ad, I drive past it sometimes and it's perfectly normal, no backstreet clinic. Several storeys high, a bit austere in the reception areas, but that's routine, also a little whiter than I like with all its tiling.

The whole thing is a Sleep Study conducted by the Laboratory for Circadian Medicine. When I consult my dictionaries I find the word *circadian* in only one place. Not in the big Webster, not in the *OED* proper, but yes in the *OED* supplement. On failing to find it—in Webster, for example—I guess, wrongly, that it's because it begins with a capital C but it doesn't. And my earlier guess that it's from some place in classical Greece, the Circades, I suppose, is also wrong. The word has a lower-case initial and is around only since 1959 and it's the invention of some genius who wants to know if some of us really live a twenty-five-hour day, some others a twenty-three-hour day, and it's made up of Latin words meaning 'about' and 'a day.'

The Study examines (I'm quoting the ad) how light exposure affects the rhythms of sleep, body temperature, and hormones, and after all those journals and monitors, participants spend up to twelve days and nights 'free of time cues' at the Laboratory. Only at this stage in the ad are we told that volunteers earn up to $750.

'Free of time cues' is really a polite name for torture, the only difference being that participants can, we hope, decide when to stop—hence the 'up to' $750.

And for further information I can call John at 555-4311—prefix 617 if I'm outside Cambridge or Boston.

———

'You have reached the Laboratory for Circadian Medicine, this is John speaking, can I help you?'

'I saw your announcement in the *Harvard Gazette*.'

'Ah yes indeed, did you wish to volunteer?'

'Well maybe but there's a few things I'd like to ask first in case—'

'Could you give me your name and address please and we'll be happy to send you an explanatory brochure —you are over sixty-five years of age?'

'Yes and under eighty-five but maybe it wouldn't even be necessary to send me the brochure and anyway it might not answer the particular question I'd like to ask—'

'Well afterwards you could—'

'But when you say up to $750, how do the volunteers work *up* to that?'

'It depends on the time they're prepared to spend in the lab—'

'No contract?'

'How do you mean?'

'I mean they don't have to spend the full twelve days—'

'Not at all, we're happy with any assistance they can give us—'

'How many earn the full $750?'

'I'm afraid I can't answer that, this is the first time this programme has been run and—'

'So you don't know how much of it they're able to stand?'

(John laughs.) 'Oh come on now, that makes it sound awful, if they're not able to stand it, as you put it, they can leave.'

'And if they leave they earn less than the $750?'

'I'm afraid so.'

————

It has to be sixty dollars a day for the twelve days and thirty dollars for your simple sleep diary and your trouble, or maybe more likely fifty dollars a day, that makes six hundred dollars, tops, and the other hundred and fifty for your sleep diary, temperature monitoring, and your trouble. On that basis, I have a hundred and fifty before I go into the lab at all.

————

Let's take food. They feed me any time I ask for it. Sorry, 'time.' If I want food, I ask for it, they give it to me. I get hungry fairly regularly, if I keep my exercise, my sleep (that's where they hope to get me), and so on in fairly even proportions. Even our dog knows the time pretty accurately by its hunger. If I let it go beyond about four o'clock in the afternoon I get a fixed laser stare from those mournful brown eyes. Why aren't we out on our walk? A thick paw laid delicately on my knee or forearm as I sit at my desk means why don't we go for our walk and have our dinner? I'm sure they've thought of all that and anyway I don't think I could practise an accurate enough logging of incipient stomach rumbles to be able to tell the time by them.

———

Ordinary plain clocks and watches and daylight are obviously out from the word go. Fairly deep breathing without strain keeps my pulse quite regular. I can guess a half-minute better than most people—by cheating. Without letting them notice, I'm taking my pulse. But a sore nuisance to be holding my wrist for twelve days and counting up to over a million. I have just got to be spotted ticking off tens or hundreds on some kind of private scorecard, I can't hold my finger to my wrist saying 'One million, two hundred and forty-four thousand, one hundred and fifty-eight, one million two hundred and forty-four thousand, one hundred and—' for each beat of my pulse because the next beat is there long before the number of the previous one is half said. And they're sure I have to sleep sometime—that's the catch and that's what they're after. But supposing I arrive at their miserable laboratory just after landing from a trans-Atlantic flight, after a twenty-nine-hour day, in fact; then I could indulge in regular sleep and fix them properly! (A disquieting afterthought—they might even let me bring in a watch and then sneak in 'at night' and fiddle the hands to fool me; but I doubt it, it's too elaborate.)

———

Maybe the toilet. 'No discomforts at all,' John says, obviously thinking of this. So I can go to the toilet whenever I like. I relieve my bladder say four or five times a day, empty the bowel once, always fairly early in the morning, I mean just about after breakfast time. This is worth working on, but first thing when I wake in the morning (see? morning?) I look at the clock, I know when it's breakfast time, and so bowel time and shower time. No clock and they have me again unless I can work it backwards, so to speak.

---

Hormones figure in their announcement, so what about sex? They probably suspect, on statistical grounds, that not many volunteers over sixty-five have a daily indulgence routine and even 'this is Saturday where's my wife (husband, partner)' isn't going to give away any clues over twelve days.

Even outside—I'm thinking like a prisoner—it's quite easy to be deceived about the days of the week. I make the mistake once in the early morning and it nags me all day. 'Christ, is this Thursday? I've the feeling all morning that it's Friday. Another day before the weekend.' Or 'God Almighty, Friday already, I'm writing Thursday on my memos all day—but it brings the weekend nearer.'

What do I do for these twelve miserable days? No, why should they be miserable? It's not as if I'm sick or something, going into a hospital for some kind of treatment; I'm doing them a favour, I'm obliging them. OK so what's not miserable about hospital nowadays—music, television, conversation? It's not a penal colony anymore. Music? Sorry. The average song lasts three and a half minutes, tapes on a cassette deck last thirty or forty-five minute a side—ideal timers. Not allowed, I bet. TV ditto. Feature film, ninety minutes, feature film plus commercials, two hours. What am I talking about? If I have TV I see the news, I know what time it is, what day it is. So no radio, no TV, no music.

Newspapers, books? A newspaper actually tells me the date, no chance; a book doesn't but I do know quite accurately how long reading takes. Eighteen hundred and fifty words, spoken at the moderate rate acceptable for a fairly serious topic on radio, I don't mean quick-fire comedy or sports commentary, eighteen hundred and fifty words fill one quarter of an hour. Reading aloud I can easily pace myself with very little practice to measure one quarter of an hour as five pages or thereabouts of a normal novel. Out too.

Conversation? Odd. They don't actually say it's out, they don't actually say you're in solitary, but I don't see how they can allow it. Volunteers can gang up on them. I count this spell, say by reciting a long poem by heart, of known duration, my mate in the next cell— sorry, ward—counts the next spell? I bet they ban conversation too.

Got it! A bad thought, actually, in the old-fashioned sense, gives it to me. Fleetingly as I consider conversation I wonder do they let husbands and wives, not to mention other couplings, volunteer together and as fleetingly I imagine the unspoken intimacies of spouses. A morning kiss. 'You need a shave.'

———

It is as white as my reconnaissance suggests—shining ceramic tiles on the lower parts of walls, silk-finish white paint above, matte white on ceilings, slightly off-white vinyl tiles on the floor, a white-covered duvet over white sheets on a white-painted hospital bed (very uncomfortable). There's a white cloth shade with an old-fashioned white silk fringe on the ceiling-centre light, an anglepoise light in white (if faintly cream) enamel. Unnecessary to state that I am entirely dependent on artificial light.

'Leave at any time,' John says, and that's about the only thing I'm free to do. If I'm free to move about too much, they say, I can go into areas lit by windows and daylight, or even areas lit by artificial light where staff work predictable and recognisable daytime shifts, so, sorry, you better stay put in this suite—'and it's not bad now, is it?'

Frankly, it isn't bad, if only I could have a radio or a newspaper to listen to or to read while I loll in this very comfortable lounge chair; and there's a rocker over there in case I feel more like a nap. (They aren't going to catch me that easily.)

I still have my secret weapon.

———

Some of the people dealing with me are what is stupidly called black. It may be beautiful but I've never seen it. I mean there's no such thing as a black person. *An fear dubh,* in Irish, the black man, is the Devil, Old Nick, Mr. Scratch, aka Beelzebub, etc., etc. It shows how completely outlandish he (or she) is. I suppose I'm sort of greyish pink. Southern Europeans tend to be slightly darker, tanned-looking is all I can really say, Maltese and northern Africans more tanned still and so on down to fairly deep brown people. So-called red Indians are less red than many a Connemara man, face aflame with sun, wind, and poitin. But nobody's really black.

I notice all this because some of the doctors or nurses or porters or paramedics or research assistants—they all just come in, perhaps at random, perhaps on a secret computerised rota—some of them are what's called black. They just come in and smile when I ring the bell and ask is it time for dinner. 'Yes of course what would you like? Today's special is a lightly grilled salmon steak served with garlic butter sauce, it comes with a tossed salad and choice of dressing: Caesar, vinaigrette, or Thousand Island—' (They know but they think I don't know that I'm asking about dinner twice in succession—I do it on purpose.)

And sometimes they come in quietly, unbidden, when I'm pretending to be asleep, and a dark visage floats between white gowns and gloves and white surgical cap, against white walls and white ceiling.

There is no mirror in my toilet suite, which is otherwise quite luxuriously appointed—in white, of course, throughout—but there is no attempt, so far as I know (the food could be drugged), to suppress my sense of touch.

I know from my practice weeks that I can rub my chin meditatively and make a shrewdly accurate estimate of the number of day's growth.

'There's plenty of hot water and stuff if you'd like to shave.'

'No thanks, I'm having a go at a beard now that I'm out of circulation for a couple of weeks.' (Up to twelve days.) Do I detect suspicion? I think not.

———

All of us volunteers—I suppose there are others somewhere—are over sixty-five and the men amongst us have an advantage over the women, even though the hospital is an equal-opportunity employer. And the women are well past any possibility of using menstrual cycles as time clues.

Let's face it, my hair is white; even those few streaks of dun we flatteringly call 'brown,' when applied to hair, are long gone; but my whiskers? Pure white for even longer than the hair, and much longer without that trace of youthful 'brown.' The strongest growth is along the jawline, just below the left- and right-hand ends of my mouth. The upper lip has a decidedly thinner crop, the sideburns almost equally so. There are patches on the high cheekbones, just below the eyes, yielding a fair product. I know all this because I'm recalling the studied experience of my practice weeks. So I also know the comparative rates of growth of these areas. They are my book of hours, my *computus,* my diary, my calendar. And my secret weapon.

------

The first week is just a breeze. Careful pacing of my normal bowel movement, morning, whatever they say, gentle rub on jaw and cheek, meaning number of days. From day seven on ($500, after all) the sideburns build up, the moustache area feels well covered at last, the jaw, as expected, begins to recall nineteenth-century generals and politicians frozen in long exposures, the patches under the eyes are bushing out in satisfactory style. But things are evening out and, despite all my precalculations, some objective check is to be desired. It is only now that I realise why there is no mirror in my toilet suite *and* no plug in the handbasin. No accident. The water surface in a full basin is a fine mirror.

------

What kind of an innocent do they think I am? There is plenty of toilet paper (I think they change the rolls when they're 'sweeping and tidying up,' as they do every 'day,' in case I'd count the sheets for tally purposes).

I unroll a mile or so of the toilet tissue and begin folding and then rolling, producing first something like a long cigarette, then something as thick as a broom handle, on to about one and a half inches, which I calculate to be the bore of the plughole. I know this tissue is highly water-soluble so speed is necessary but this does for a tryout anyway. Paper plug into plughole, tap on, so far so good. Basin fills up, tap off, let it settle, there below me mirrored in the flat surface is the sheen of the white tiles over the handbasin, illuminated by the ceiling-centre light of my toilet suite.

Unfortunately, as I lean over narcissistically to look at my face in my clever mirror, I cast my own shadow over the whole basin; the light is falling on the back of my head and I see nothing except the vague varied whiteness of water under borrowed light and a disintegrating wad of toilet tissue. Never mind.

There is over the handbasin another light fixture, fitted with a socket to accept an electric razor, unused of course. There is in my pocket a Swiss army knife with eight possible extensions—large blade, small blade, keyhole saw, screwdriver, can opener, corkscrew, piercing blade, and tiny screwdriver neatly twisted into the whorls of the corkscrew. No problem then to undo the courtesy light-fitting over the basin and pull it out to the end of a fortunate couple of feet of its cord stuffed behind its paneling, then manoeuvre it between water and face. Sorry, no water. The rolled tissue is turned to pulp and is away in the drains somewhere.

More winding, insert paper plug, turn on tap, water surface rises, turn off tap. Take lamp in left hand, hold it between face and water.

———

I see nothing. The white sideburns blend with the white Dundrearies, with the white beard, the white moustache, the sprouting white mass below the eyes, the white eyebrows, the white hair, the white tiles behind, the white ceiling above, the white light, the deliquescent mush of the white toilet paper, all one.

There are no time clues and I am simply plunging my left hand, lamp and all, into the basin of water. Free of time.

# Dead Lines

When the circular came from the Minister for Health I was able to reply truthfully that apart from the invisibly disabled like myself we had on the staff one definitely certifiably recognisable handicapped person. I omitted to mention that he was in fact far better at doing his job than many of his allegedly advantaged or abled or scratch colleagues. I referred to our blind telephonist John Lyons. When any of his sighted substitutes took his place on his day off, their confusion in front of the mass of numbers, jacks, dipping extension markers, and red and black switches made the telephone system even worse than usual.

When John Lyons was on the switchboard, things went as well as they could, given the inbuilt faults of the system. He it was who gave me a very useful tip. You can test your own appliance for faults in a minor sort of way and even clear them.

Suppose that your phone is failing to get you through to the person to whom you wish to speak. The fault could be at your end, somewhere in the middle, or at the far end. The middle is of course a ferocious mess of wires, relays, switch-gears automatic and manual, jack plugs, sockets, printed circuits, and microchips for all I know, and only an expert dare undertake a repair job in that jungle. But the amount of stuff at either end is relatively small and uncomplicated, and minor faults in these sections when detected can be nearly self-correcting. Thus when you fail to get out, so to speak, you wonder where the fault is. You can in fact determine if your own end is functioning properly by the simple procedure of dialing your own number. If your appliance is in good order, it will yield the conventional engaged tone. If it is not, you will get one of the assortment of whistles, clicks, dings, bubbles, whines, hisses, hums, chatters, and howls which enter the system from the wires, relays, et cetera, already recited at more than tedious length. Or you may land in the innocent centre of a conversation, always interminable and always unintelligible, between other parties.

There is one slight bonus. If you do manage to get your own number to yield the engaged tone, you may find that in the process of ringing it you have given a nudge to whatever slight irregularity at your end may have caused the original malfunction; try again for your first-sought number and with luck you may have healed yourself and may get out successfully.

Never content to let well enough alone, of course I had to try it immediately. My home phone number is 889586. I picked up the instrument, listened for the steadily purring ready signal, dialed 889586, and was delighted to find that John's account was borne out in every particular. I heard my own phone, nestling there on my shoulder, telling me with a high peep-peep over and over again that it—I—was busy.

I hope the Minister for Health was happy to learn that we provide a job for a blind citizen. His colleague the Minister for Posts and Telegraphs is probably less happy to know that the telephone service might as well be provided only to citizens who are stone-deaf. I was, accordingly, never short of opportunities for trying my new trick.

It worked well enough until one day I got not an engaged tone but the ringing tone normal for an outgoing call. Had I dialed wrong? I paused a moment, deciding to try it again, but did not cut off quickly enough to prevent my hearing the click of a lifted telephone at the other end and a voice muttering (I could have sworn) '889586.' I dialed again, with special care on the third and fourth figures. It must have been '59' I had heard, with only the diphthongs *i* sounding clearly. This time I again heard the sound of a phone ringing instead of the expected engaged tone, but I waited. Again the click of a handset lifting, a pause, and a slightly sharper voice, more clear than muttering, '889586.'

'I'm sorry,' I said, 'I must have the wrong number. I was trying to dial myself.' I realised immediately how silly it sounded, though not so silly as the response. 'Who do you think you're talking to?' This was followed by a laugh or snigger or something between, neither 'ha-ha' (in the conventional notation) nor yet quite 'heh-heh-heh.' With a hasty finger I jabbed down the stud which disconnected my lines, replaced the receiver slowly, and sat wondering.

Two days later I was again failing to get a call through successfully and again resorted to the blind telephonist's trick. This time the voice came quick and clear: '889586.' 'I was just trying to clear my lines,' I said; 'if you dial your own number you should get an engaged tone if your own lines are OK and then you can start again. I rang 889586.' There was a pause and a reply from the other end: 'Of course I know the voice. What do you want?' I rang off again quickly and decided I had had enough of this nonsense. There wasn't even any way I could make an intelligible complaint to the supervisor.

For a good while thereafter my phone behaved quite normally. My teenage daughter carried on her long jerky conversations with girlfriends about boyfriends. People called me to advise me of committee meetings or chess matches. My wife was begged by phone at short notice to teach extra courses; she thought about it for a while, rang back to accept, and got through without difficulty.

The other event—I suppose there has to be another event or there wouldn't be a story, if a story is an account of a connected series of events—the other event happened miles away from the spooky phone, in the damp flat midlands with their tame canals.

I had just driven through Allenwood, at the beginning of a long straight on the road toward Dublin. Allenwood was always good for a smile, as I glanced around to see if William Carroll's decoration of his shop-front had faded enough to reveal his earlier sign: 'self-service WILLIAM CARROLL undertaker.' Though evening was closing in, there was still enough light to see that the overpainting of the unconscious joke was still surviving.

The straight road toward Prosperous stretched before me through light young forestry, and occasional cars and pedestrians passed in both directions. Traffic, such as it was, was even thinner when I was about midway between the two villages. I speeded up slightly and a stupid dark brown donkey stepped out, backwards it seemed, from a dark brown hedgerow and stopped right in front of me. I braked and swerved and the donkey did a half-scamper sideways with his hindquarters; my four-letter exclamation and the thump of my front wing on his backside coincided. The dumb thing cantered off, or whatever donkeys do, and after showing a slight stagger for a few paces got back into a normal donkey pace and disappeared into the growing dark brown evening. Meanwhile I had manoeuvred the car back to its proper side of the road and pulled in. I got out and examined the front wing and saw that there was a notable dinge surrounded by cracked varnish. Knowing that my insurance company would never bother to seek out and sue the owner of a stray donkey, I just got into the car again and drove on.

Not much of an event, but that's only half the second event. I mean, how many events are there in blowing my nose? I put my hand in my pocket, take out my hanky, raise my hand, blow, wipe, return hanky, and so on—how many events? Anyway, it was in growing darkness I approached Prosperous, and a slightly denser traffic of people and cars caused me to slow behind another car. Suddenly a staggering man flopped from the narrow grass verge against the side of the car in front, bounced crazily off its wing and along it, twisted with another heavy bounce off the rear wing, and fell crazily spreadeagled on the roadway under my front bumper as I jerked to a stop, almost standing on my brakes, and the taillights of the car in front faded in the darkness.

My hands and knees trembled in jiggling shock as I got out, my cheeks flattened tightly over my clamped jaws; there was a cold vacancy in the pit of my stomach. I knelt beside the splayed figure and knew immediately that he was dead. The face was broken and splashed with blood and the head was at an angle which was an insult to humanity.

My vacant mind hunted in every direction, instantly dazzled by the horrifying possibility that nothing would be seen by anyone except the corpse lying awry under my bumper and the donkey-dinge in my left front wing.

That's enough of an event for me any day and twenty minutes later I was at a telephone in the back parlour of a pub in Prosperous, breathing deeply, pantingly, sipping a large whiskey. I dialed home with a still-quivering finger. 'Hey,' I blurted out when the first sound of a lifted phone and a 'hello' began at the other end, 'something desperate has happened, and I don't know what the hell I'm going to do.' There was none of the hurried response in expectation of which I had built my opening sentence. A dulling and familiar voice replied at the end of the pause. 'Oh, trouble? An accident?' My throat tightened for speech but no words were available. 'Will you for Christ's sake get off my line? You're always getting in my bloody way. I rang my own number.' 'And what do you think you've got? Weren't you calling home to tell about an accident? Maybe to look for help or advice? Tell me.'

The tightened muscles around my ribs and stomach relaxed a fraction, though the cold still held on about me. My hunched shoulders dropped an easing inch. 'Look,' I said, 'a drunk flopped against a car in front of me killed himself and finished up almost under my front wheels. I know he was drunk because the smell of whiskey off him would knock you flat. But the other car drove on, maybe they didn't even know about it, though I don't see how they could've avoided knowing with that bang.' 'Maybe they didn't know they'd hit a man.' 'That's exactly it, they might've thought they'd hit a donkey.' 'A donkey?' 'Well, I'd bumped into a donkey myself a couple of minutes earlier and now there I was sitting stopped with a dead man under my bumper and a fresh dinge on my left front wing though I hadn't touched him but who'd believe that?' 'Is it a moral or a legal problem?' 'What do you mean? I don't know. What's it got to do with me morally?' 'Nothing much perhaps except that you happened to be there.' 'That wasn't my fault either.' 'I didn't say fault, but why do you feel guilty or whatever it is? Did you call the police?' 'No, because of that stupid donkey dinging my wing.' 'So you called your own number only, to report home that something desperate had happened. You could even have called a lawyer.' 'What good is a lawyer to me and what did I do. . . .' 'I don't know what you did to need a lawyer but if you do, you must have done something you think somebody will think you should feel guilty about.'

My muscles were tightened up again and a faint lightness and tingling were spreading through my torso and limbs. My knee jerked up and down with a quivering intensity. My voice came high-pitched: 'And what about that bastard in front, why didn't he stop?' 'Did you get his number?' 'How the hell could I get his number when all I was thinking was would I hit the fellow who'd just bounced off that car in front and was collapsing under my front wheels?' 'And where is he now?'

I paused, limp and light all over with frustration and unmerited guilt. 'I bundled him into the ditch and came on to the nearest place to ring home. But he was dead I tell you.'

There was a click and then silence and then the renewed tiny purring noise which fizzes over telephone lines round the inhabited globe of the world. He was lying out there with blood drying on his face, warmth ebbing from his body into the stones and clay of the soft road margin, totally devoid of humanity since those impacts had wrenched his neck to that impossible and destroying angle. My line home was dead too.

## Vacancy for a Photo-finisher

For thirty years, from the age of eighteen onward, I weighed just under eleven and a half stone. Then, fairly suddenly, my weight rose to just under twelve and stayed there no matter what I did. Not that I did much. I walked a bit more, cycled to work a couple of times a week instead of the ritual once a month I always did anyway in honour of the sanctity of the human bicycle. Now and again I declined a gooey oversweet dessert. There was little point in doing or avoiding anything until I discovered what had caused the sudden increase and this I was unable to do. I concluded eventually that some new and uncontrollable factor had entered my life, perhaps a function of the passage of time. The further conclusion seemed perfectly obvious: I must introduce a new but controllable counterfactor.

I tried jogging, but the thump of my blurred feet below me on the hard road became excessively boring after a few outings. (They were blurred because I cannot wear my glasses when running.) I gave up so soon that my running shorts had not even become soiled enough to need washing. They lay in a corner of the wardrobe and only when their faint aroma grew more rancid did I decide that they probably needed washing after all.

I tried yoga. The teacher had a Dublin accent and you can hardly call a chap with a Dublin accent a guru. When I entered the hall where the instruction was given, I got a faint whiff of running shorts. He told us we were about to cleanse our bodies. I wondered why he didn't say 'clean,' because obviously I have nothing against bathing, but this isn't what he was after at all. 'There was a lady here took the course,' he said, 'older than you, way out of condition she was, flabby all over, but at the end of the second session she brought up a whole basinful of pure yellow, great.' At the end of the first session I felt an acid touch at the back of my throat and left as quickly as I decently could.

I decided that the old motto 'mens sana in corpore sano,' a sound mind in a healthy body, was widely misunderstood. I did not understand why I should imagine that it means physical fitness will improve the mind, when it might just as well mean that a fit mind will make your body healthy. I gave up physical jerks and kept a lookout for psychical jerks instead. They are more frequent than I used to think.

From the window of a plane banking and turning to land at Chicago I saw the lights of the city laced out on a vertical cliff beside me instead of below me. There was no lurch against the seat belt, tight against my thick midriff, no disorientation of the body. Upright remained straight above my head. The black lake, the lakeshore drive, and the skyscrapers of glass and concrete blazing with light were a mural instead of a carpet. I seemed to be inside one of those trick pictures in which you cannot decide whether you are looking at the upper or lower surfaces of the treads and risers of a staircase, until you impose the power of your own eye on the drawing and make it turn upside down or back to front or inside out as you wish.

In the airport terminal I saw a fat lady in late middle age bounding down a stairs in great six-foot leaps. I cheat, actually, in telling it that way but only as I was cheated in the event. I was waiting at a baggage delivery bay and happened to glance up. Nearby was the solid balustrade of a staircase and over the balustrade I could see this lady, or at least her head and hefty shoulders, her bulging torso and plump arms. She was descending, as I have said, in great bounds. I knew that Americans take their senior citizens very seriously and that the senior citizens consequently take themselves very seriously and cultivate fitness and activity in a way that effete Europeans would consider ridiculously energetic. I also knew that the middle-aged American woman has a highly developed adipose complex. Nevertheless I never expected to see a sexagenarian performing acrobatics in public. I collected my bag and moved toward the staircase to ascend to the next level. When I had passed the obscuring balustrade and reached the foot of the stairs I saw that it was the downward half of an escalator. The gentlest steps taken by the lady had been invisibly accelerated into the standing leaps by which the devil came into Athlone.

My journey was continued by rail, and as I sat in the train awaiting its departure I had an attack of that illusory sense of motion which is a commonplace for train travelers. I have often experienced it myself when sitting in a train or even a bus at rest, flanked by another train or bus. There is sudden panic as, ahead of its time, the train begins to move. Even though I know quite well what is happening I have to remind myself that it is not my train but the other one which is moving. All the little adjustments have taken place throughout my body which would have been proper if it were in fact my train which was moving—shifting of the backside on the seat, slight tensing of the shoulders, a movement of the head backward or forward. Everything in the foreground is still: me, the seats, the carriage's window frame. That frame is filled with the total background (the other train), and there is no point of reference to tell me which train is in motion.

My immediate surroundings fit me as a glove does, firmly up against my skin. They share my upness and downness, my leftness and rightness, my forwards and backwards. I must look away, to the other static and immobile platform, to re-reverse a silly reversal.

Later the train bore me southward across the immense prairie of Illinois. The track was in a dead straight line, often paralleled by a nearby and equally straight highway. In autumn this landscape is one of America's fields of waving grain; now, in the darkening winter evening, it was a featureless flat expanse of white snow. My fellow passengers slumped quietly dozing; the noise of wheels was an undifferentiated purr. Oblong patches of light from the windows fell on the undifferentiated whiteness of the snow. I raised my eyes and saw the headlights of a car on the adjoining highway. These lights too fell onto bare whiteness of packed snow on the roadway. I and the train, the illuminated patches of white snow and the car headlamps, were locked in a single system within which there was no evidence of movement.

Slowly and eerily the car began to reverse toward the rear of the train. Suddenly another car shot past in the opposite direction and destroyed my quiet mental picture with obtrusive new evidence of space, speed, and direction. Instantaneously I was warped back to their conventional disposition.

It was all very upsetting. In the plane, I was moving at a hundred miles an hour or so and the geological earth reared up beside me. In the stationary train I was rock-steady and the moving train alongside induced the feeling of movement within me. Now in the moving train, a moving car beside me held me still.

A week or so later I flew home and arrived for breakfast at the end of a day of only eighteen hours. Breakfast should of course be at the beginning of the day and six vanished hours turned dinner into morning coffee. For a few days I could not eat properly and woke up hungry in the middle of the night. Typical jet lag.

Once I woke in pitch darkness to the sound of heavy distant hammering. Someone was wielding a sledge-hammer outside on the road, I guessed about thirty yards away, probably trying to break a hole in the pavement outside Cronins' or Leonards', across the road from us. Each metallic bang of the hammer was followed by a die-away series of minor pinging noises as the hammer bounced. It was perfectly regular and as it continued without interruption and with no murmur of accompanying talk of workmen, moving of shovels, car engines, nothing but the BANG-Bang-ting-ting, BANG-Bang-ting-ting, I wondered was my first impression wrong. If an emergency job were being done on a gas or water main or an ESB cable, surely there would be more commotion. I sat up, intending to go out to investigate, and suddenly, with the change of my position, the whole perspective of the event changed. The sound now came from below me and it was not a loud hammering muted by distance, it was close by but faint—the breathing of my wife lying beside me asleep. A little uvular snag at the point of address to each expiration was the BANG, a slight wheeze was the Bang-ting-ting.

At least this night starvation might be doing my weight some good. Had I gone faster and farther, a quarter of a great circle would have had me ninety degrees out of plumb and walking up the walls.

Back at work, I chatted to colleagues of the tall sky-scrapers and the vast plains though my most abiding secret memories were of those distortions of space and time. 'OK, OK,' the boss said, 'back to your grindstones, chaps, you can get the rest of the traveler's tales on your own time, not the firm's. And I've a new job for you, someone has just left in a load of old stereo negs for treatment.'

I was a finisher in a large photographic D & P station. I had begun on simple negative work, spotting out with opaque the tiny pinholes left in negatives by faulty processing. These, if uncorrected, would print as unwanted black dots in the positives. Useful work, involving some skill, but deadly boring. I was moved on to work with prints, shading in unwanted highlights with a fine spray of microscopic dots or supplying glinting highlights in portraits' eyes. Sometimes more drastic work was done on prints, but this would be when they were being prepared for re-copying, for making new negatives from which the final positive prints would be made.

I learnt to view negative and positive with equal ease, much as a hotel receptionist learns to read upside down as his guests sign the register in front of him, or as a printer indeed learns to read both upside down and backwards as he checks the sorts in his stick. I amused or infuriated my colleagues with a project for a grand revolutionary film on racial tension.

The parts of blacks would be played by whites, the parts of whites by blacks, and the film would be released in negative prints. The incidental music would be played from scores placed upside down on the lecterns, treble become bass, bass become treble, and the last bar, or a reversal of it, become the first. And to make lack of assurance doubly unsure, the recordings would be played backwards.

I once learnt by heart a song which I heard backwards through the accidental change from one tape recorder to another. The text is of some interest to alienists, philologists, and musicologists.

Zray rui mad law zrizwal vona ger ruid law
Es na niush ne haydn law masser mee niam o
Law masser law masser minyam
Law masser law masser minyam o.

Now, however, I was being moved up again, and to a better class of real work, almost archival work, the examination and conservation of old glass plates. And these were no ordinary plates. It would have taken me some time to realise that they were the 'old stereo negs' the boss had spoken of so lightly.

As only a few will ever have had the opportunity to familiarise themselves with this exotic photographic genre, the many are entitled to some explanation of what I'm talking about.

The brass and mahogany stereoscope was a feature of Victorian drawing rooms and the stereogram is a picture which is even more illusory than most. The extra illusion is that of depth or the so-called third dimension. A photographic stereogram was made by exposing two pictures of the same subject at the same time in a twin-lens camera. The lenses were mounted side by side, like a pair of human eyes. The plate on development showed two square pictures side by side, differing only, and very slightly, in their angle of view, one a left-eye view, the other a right-eye view. Prints from this pair of pictures were mounted side by side in a small box or frame and viewed through twin eyepieces like those of a pair of binoculars. Left eye saw the left-eye view, right eye saw the right-eye view, and the two views coalesced, somewhat as in the real-life experience of seeing, and separated into clear layers of foreground, middle ground, and background. In fact, anyone with a little practice can easily learn to adjust the accommodation and focus of the eyes to experience the illusion of depth in a stereo pair without benefit of apparatus. Strangely enough there is no way I can prove or demonstrate to anyone else that I have had this experience, with or without the apparatus. It is an adjustment of the optical process inside my head and I can only state that it has happened.

There is a further point of explanation which is unfortunately necessary. The image in a camera is inverted. When your old-fashioned photographer draped his head and his camera in a black cloth to focus and compose the image on his ground-glass screen, the image he saw was upside down and backwards, sky at the bottom, confirmation class of 1936 at the top, the date on the chalked board in the middle reading 9ε6Ⅰ. No problem, of course, it's all done with mirror images and comes out perfectly clear and correct in the print. The double image of a stereo pair is however ⊥ℲƎ⅃ ⊥HפIꓤ and if I invert a straight print of this I get RIGHT LEFT and my left eye will be seeing the right-eye view! So I must cut the print into its two halves and invert them separately to get LEFT RIGHT.

I had no diamond or authority to slice our customer's antique glass plates in two and had to accustom myself to the examination of the integrated negative.

The foregoing tedious explanation has been necessary to establish the situation in which I underwent the psychical jerk to beat all. The stereo negative gives the illusion of depth all right but everything is back to front. The featureless background hills, grey lumps on the skyline, were foreground flats, the work of a perverse set designer. The foreground peasant was, with sharpest detail, in the far background, through a peas-ant-shaped window in the hills.

Among the first batch of plates I examined was a picture of Ireland's most photographed subject, the Giant's Causeway. No serried ranks here of basalt columns receding into the distance but hollow hexagonal pigeonholes reaching out at me. It was a triumph of mind over matter or matter over mind, depending literally on how I looked at it.

Hollow and solid are clearly as interchangeable as black and white, up and down, in and out, static and mobile, forward and backward. The cure for that slight waistline bulge was within my grasp; it needed only an effort of concentration and will.

I paused by my front gate with my hand on its cold, black iron bars and tried to reverse the world. Let solid be hollow, vacant be solid. My hand and the gate were empty vacant spaces, gaps in vast solidity, like bubbles underwater; but air bubbles underwater move too fast and too fizzily, I couldn't capture and pin down the image.

There are modern drawing room ornaments which suit my purpose better. Cylindrical glass bowls of translucent coloured fluid are lit and warmed from below by an electric lamp. A convection current is set up and it moves the fluid about, shifting with it the shapes and positions of a few viscid globs of oil. A hard effort of imagination could even endow a bubble now and again with embryonic limbs and head and I could see it as something like a remotely human shape, waving its little blobby roots of arms, kicking slowly its blobby little roots of legs.

As my hand grasped the cold iron, a better figure occurred to me, a vision of a shaped toy balloon, with the configuration of a twisted rope, perhaps, or a dog or a teddy bear or a Mickey Mouse. There are even balloons which can be inflated and then pulled and twisted into all kinds of shapes, travesties of human and animal forms. The thin rubber skin of such a balloon is the barest possible frontier between its empty interior, a mere shaped space, and everything outside. Vacancy without and within at least brought into equilibrium, if not yet fully reversed. Cut into a loaf of bread and find a hole in it. This hole is the shaped space of a balloon interior. At last I had it.

I looked at my hand against the railings and saw tubes there, not the sleeves of my shirt, jacket, and raincoat, but the skin of my arms and fingers. These tubes too were a frontier between the vacancy within and the crusted solidity outside, what people thinking the other way would call the empty air. The black paint of the railing was a frontier too and as the railing itself could be indifferently a tube or a bar depending on how I looked at it, I opted for tube. I mentally eroded its metal rim and paint into a thinner and thinner membrane which ultimately vanished and left only tube-shaped hollowness in the surrounding massivity.

The weight of massive and brutal material pressed my ethereal hand and the tenuous railing together. However thin the immateriality of hand and rail, the surface between them was unyielding and when I pressed I felt the sharp snagging of a protruding sliver of iron or a vitrified fleck of paint on the outer mantle of my hand and I gasped with the sudden pain. When my hands were solid, they would have been pierced, a drop of blood would have oozed out, but now the subtle rarity of my hollowness was being attacked and nothing was running out. Knotted and clotted lumpishness of matter was squeezing my exhausted limb.

My fingers contracted and I could see soft wrinkles and folds appear as the skin loosened, a dying Christmas balloon on Saint Stephen's Day, now too large for the straightening space within. I felt my shoes loosen too and looking down saw my socks collapsing round my shrinking ankles, a gap growing between sock and shoe. Paralysing limpness relaxed the outer shells of my body; I could feel soft bulges remaining irregularly here and there about me as the cave-in accelerated.

The trousers slackened round my waist at last and fell to the floor. Jacket, shirt, and vest slipped from the vanishing shoulders and joined the formless heap where I had been standing. I saw them for a fraction of a second before everything went black. Then there were two soft plops, which must have been the eyes going, so the ears must have survived the longest.

## Meruleus Lacrimans

M iss Eveleen was only seventy-nine; she was small and growing smaller. Her sister Norah was eighty-two and could grow no smaller without vanishing. It was Miss Eveleen who came eventually in response to the policeman's knocking. He could barely hear the slow clack-clack of her loose shoes on the linoleum.

The upper panel of the hall door was made of many pieces of glass: there were leaded strips of green and red and diamond-shaped small panes the colour of dark honey, all around the edge. The main light was clear glass, thick, and greyed with the clouded bubbles of its imperfections. The kitchen door too had a glass panel and the gleam of its light filtered up the two steps at the back of the hallway, passed the bottom of the stairs and the dining room door, passed the looped-back curtain which partitioned front from back, mingled with the rainbow hues from the front door.

When Miss Eveleen had come to the doorway of the dining room and peered along the hall, there was a moving pattern of dark patches on the front door's glass. She took a few shuffling steps forward and some of the patches coalesced into a rough silhouette of head and shoulders. As she passed the hallstand she glanced in the mirror. Dust on the mirror and on her spectacles deepened the gloom—the dirt and disarray were invisible.

She had in her turn obscured the faint light from the kitchen door but the civic guard in the porch could identify nothing. He knocked again and she took a few further steps. The door opened to the short length of its protective chain and he saw a little old lady in long dark clothes. Strands of her thin hair draggled below her round hat of black plaited straw. Her face was misshapen, her cheeks hollowed into the gaps between her teeth. Her eyes were wide, magnified by the thick lenses, and stared out from a reticulation of dark lines on her skin, a tracery of dirt-filled wrinkles.

A modesty vest of greyed lace was below her throat; the points of a shawl of black shiny stuff with greenish sheen were held together at her breast by a brooch. It was a stamped shape of base metal and chips of diamanté crystal still gleamed faintly in a few of its tiny sockets.

'No, thank you, my brother will be calling shortly.'

'Yes, m'm, but the ladies in the Legion asked—'

'Thank you,' she interrupted, 'the ladies are very kind but my brother will be calling shortly.' She closed the door, scraping it across a litter of brown envelopes on the floor.

She turned away from the door and faced back into the house. It was a nice house, two-storey with return, brick fronted, other walls in rubble masonry cement rendered. Perfectly suitable for a prosperous furniture merchant, J. & P. Montgomery and Sons, Winetavern Street. Pappa (accented on the last syllable) was the last of the sons and he bought the house near the turn of the century when they were tall girls in long frocks. She shuffled back to the dining room, where they lived. 'A young policeman,' she said, and her sister nodded slowly, 'but I told him Roland is coming.'

When Norah had tripped on the rotted fronds of the stair carpet she had cut her leg and barely reached her chair again in safety. The wound and bruise were on her calf, on the site of a knotted varicose vein. A slow and lingering ulcer grew around it, fringed with glossy yellow and bluish brown. Stairs were dangerous and the remote upper storeys—Pappa's and Mamma's bedroom, the small return rooms, all beyond the first landing with its toilet—all disappeared.

Pappa was on the cold white marble mantelpiece, a photograph in a frame of folded tin covered in blackening oilcloth. The glass over the photograph was dulled by spots of airborne organic dirt and the mould it nourished. The highlights of the photograph bleached whiter and whiter, the sepia faded to dim smudges of eye sockets, moustache, the line of the lips. Behind him wide flowers in the wallpaper pattern had faded too and the wall was a reach of mottled dull cream.

When she sat down, though slowly, the seat of Eveleen's chair shifted another fraction of an inch with an unheard squeak. A few fibres drifted to the floor from the edge of a bare patch on the figured velvet. A pinch of parched wooddust drifted with it from worm-raddled dowelling.

The policeman went back to the car, got in, and slammed the door in exasperation. 'Christ Almighty,' he exclaimed, 'you should've seen all the bloody letters on the floor, bet half them are from the shaggin' solicitor.'

'Roland will be coming soon, Norah, shall I make a cup of tea?' Norah nodded barely and Eveleen went carefully from the dining room to the hall. She glanced toward the hall door; its coloured glazing was uncompromised. She went down two steps with separate stiff movements of her ankles, knees, and hips and entered the kitchen.

The back door led from the kitchen to the yard but the back door had become swollen and soft, its weatherboard scraped and jammed on the yard's granite slab. The shudders finally pulled the hinge-screws from the pulpy wood and the door was hanging useless, a barrier. The yard, the garden, and the back lane disappeared.

On each side of the chimney breast in the kitchen there was a doorway, one to the scullery and one to the small narrow room where the maid used to sleep. There was always a maid from the country, a strong girl with red arms, black hair, and a strange accent. Once there was a girl from Kerry who spoke Irish. The maid did the heavy work, carrying buckets of coal from the shed, hefting bins of rubbish to the back lane.

The scullery still existed, part of the little track—scullery, kitchen, hall, dining room, toilet—to which the house had shrunk. Eveleen took the teapot from the gas stove, brought it into the scullery, and emptied its stale wad of leaves into the sink.

The maid's room had vanished, its door closed forever. Its one small window had broken, squeezed and strained by the press of rampant bushes in the garden, stretched and contracted by sun and frost. Damp dust accumulated on the floor inside it and there a bleached sycamore seedling grew, a stunted waif. On that wall of the maid's room which backed on the kitchen there was a splay of water pipes, an inexpert plumber's afterthought. Old lead and tinsmith's special on bulby wipe joints weathered and fatigued and droplets of water oozed through. Dust mould of rot blew in and about and found a habitat. The dust particles were myriad though invisible and could easily bear the attrition of the years. In a warm early summer the survivors stirred and began to multiply, slowly at first. A yellow-grey patch spread with an outer rim of dark lines, a map, perhaps, or a diagram of a distant nebula. Then the centre opened out with faint tints of blue and pink and grew a downy meadow of a million lightest hairlets. Each bore a tear of deadly distilled liquor which wept, dried, blew its dust further, established new colonies, burrowed through the friable brick, mortar, and plaster of the kitchen chimney breast. A grotesque sacred heart grew on the wall over the cavern which held the cold and rusty iron range. *Meruleus lacrimans.*

When the water in the teapot boiled she put into it two teaspoonfuls of leaves, stirred, and stood waiting.

They were waiting for Roland or Ronan. Roland was younger and did not remember living over the shop. He was a great Irishian and as Ronan Mac Cneamhaire played one tune on the warpipes and wore a kilt in the Gaelic League's annual Saint Patrick's Day parade.

He was a friend to the great, Mr. de Valera knew him well. It was to him that Mr. de Valera presented the trowel with which the aging president laid the first brick at the commencement of the reconstruction of the library of Trinity College. It was Ronan who had given the speech introducing the president at the opening and dedication of the Garden of Remembrance and Ronan had afterward presented the key used on this occasion to the patriotic museum in Kilmainham Gaol. He clung to his image of Mr. de Valera's image of him. He pushed himself forward as firmly as his fading body and the bemused aide-de-camp would allow to grasp the hand of the near-blind statesman as soon as possible after the death of Mrs. de Valera, to draw new sustenance from that hand, speaking strongly to identify himself. 'It's Ronan, Chief, Ronan Mac Cneamhaire. We're all terribly sorry about poor Sinéad, but she had a great life, a great life. Ar dheis Dé go raibh sí.' 'Cé h-é sin, cé h-é sin?' asked de Valera, 'ó, tusa, go raibh maith agat, go raibh maith agat.'

When Mr. de Valera lay on a deathbed Ronan sat slumped at home with staring eyes in a drawn face. His daughter-in-law called in the morning to say hello and make him a cup of tea and found him with his face twisted in the spasm of cardiac infarction. The radio was still talking but merely summarising the rest of the news at the end of a bulletin which had been devoted to the career, illness, and death of the ex-president. He had become part of the memorable, the imaginable, the still known. Ronan had vanished.

The station sergeant had an elbow on a ledger open at the day's entries for stolen cars. 'I know, Father, I know,' he said into the telephone, 'I know but what on earth can we do? . . . OK, I suppose we'll have to eventually. Yeah, I'll let you know how we get on.' He nodded to the young guard who raised his eyes with a grimace. 'The old ladies on the Avenue?' he asked, knowing the answer in advance.

With a coarse leather gardening glove on his clenched right fist the young guard struck hard at the centre of the upper panel of the hall door. The sheet of plain glass shattered, the coloured strips and diamond shapes around the edge hung in the slots of their leading. He reached through and disengaged the protective chain, then opened the door. He kicked aside the damp envelopes lying on the floor and walked down the dim hallway. In the big room to his right he saw on the mantelpiece a blank white card behind a spotted glass in a frame of folded tin covered with dark oilcloth. There was a coating of dust on the floor, wood-fluff, fibres from the velvet upholstery, fragments of cotton and wool, satin, and lace.

In the kitchen, between mounds of old newspapers, there was a pathway of sorts, leading past the gas stove toward the scullery. On the stove was a teapot full of cold tea. On the tiled floor in front of the stove, greasy dust lay thick. There were wisps of carbon blown and rolled over years from the jets, there were double-digested flecks of breadcrumbs, of tea leaves, chewed, excreted, re-ingested, re-excreted, by generations of foul if tiny organisms.

Of the poor misfortunate ould bitches there was no sign at all.

## Swopping Bikes

Teenagers of the Inuit, so I read in my anthropology books, entertain their younger siblings by story-knifing. The knife is a sharpened bone of whale or walrus or seal and with this they draw swift sketches in the sand to illustrate successive phases of the stories they tell to the little ones. And as swiftly erase them to make room for the next sketch. It is a simple form of cinema, or at least of the storyboard which serves as a sketchpad for the filmmaker or comic-strip artist.

———

I lost my memory once. Not all of my memory, of course, just the bit relating to one particular part of my past. Come to think of it, it's not quite accurate to say I lost my memory because I'm not sure I ever had it.

———

It was in the great bicycle age, the years during the war when we reigned on the roads. An odd army or turf lorry here and there, an odd doctor's car on a suburban road, buses or trams on main roads up to nine o'clock in the evening—these were all that challenged us. Our rolling stock was pretty run down by the time the war ended, bald tyres were lined with other bald tyres from which the wire rims had been removed, aged tubes were rendered less porous by having a little milk poured in through the valve neck, to swirl round and (it was hoped) form a healing skin on the old and perishing rubber.

―――――

Mutual exchange of bicycles in motion between consenting adults was, even in those unregenerate days, not considered a felony, save insofar as prohibited in general terms by the Road Traffic Act, rather than the Criminal Law Amendment Act. It was this exchange which was the climax of our achievement. It would have made a good circus act, if a circus could have been organised on a gentle three-quarter-mile slope instead of in the conventional rings.

Protracted searching had finally revealed Belmont Avenue as the ideal location. It is still a quiet residential suburban road, but it is no longer empty of cars, as it then was. Now they are parked on both sides and must weave carefully in a narrow lane between ranks of their parked fellows, upslope to Sandford or downslope to Donnybrook. Then it was clear, empty, available.

―――――

The method was fairly simple and involved only two basic skills and two critical unrehearsable moments of risk. And one of the skills is so common that it's hardly worth mentioning—merely the ability to skip onto and off a bicycle, to and from either side. Perhaps I should be more specific: it must be done in the male manner, that is, with the leg swinging over the saddle from behind. And at least one of the bicycles must be of the male persuasion, with a crossbar. This skill of skipping on has to have a slight elaboration added.

There is a moment, during the skipping on, when I have one foot (the off foot) on a pedal as I freewheel, the other (really the near foot) trailing below and behind as it waits to swing up and over the saddle. I must learn to switch these fast as I freewheel, and freewheel with the near foot on the pedal, for example with the right foot on the left pedal or the left foot on the right pedal.

The second skill is the ability, while sitting on the crossbar of one bike, to steer an empty bike alongside by holding one of its handlebars. This skill was in fact forced upon us, particularly on the girls, by the material conditions of the time. In those days, bike-mending was regarded as an exclusively male privilege or duty and girls' bikes tended to be less well maintained and more liable to puncture or other breakdown. Many a girl had to welcome a crossbar home from her boyfriend and while sitting on his crossbar had to stretch out a hand to pilot her own punctured crock bumping and trundling alongside.

———

OK. Paddy and I set off down Belmont Avenue in line abreast. I was First Person and on the left. I began skipping off toward Paddy but delayed in midskip, so to speak, freewheeling (now the need for the long slow downhill is obvious), and did the foot-change routine on the pedal nearest Paddy. I was now free to reach out my right foot toward Paddy's bike while he obligingly left his left pedal free for me to engage my right foot on it. Still steering my own bike, I gently eased my weight onto Paddy's left pedal, then eased my backside onto his crossbar—he again obligingly taking his left hand off its handlebar to give me access.

Now I was in the position of the girl with the stricken bike being given a crossbar home by the boyfriend, sitting on Paddy's crossbar while I steered my empty bike alongside. Paddy began the skip-off routine toward my empty bike, switched feet on the pedal of his own bike on the side nearest my bike, reached out with his off (free) foot and engaged it on the empty near pedal of my bike, eased his weight and control over to it, then (the nasty moment this) abandoned full control of his bike to me, on its crossbar, while I abandoned control of my bike to him at the same instant. Now the bikes separated and it was merely a matter for each of us to adopt a more normal posture and proceed—I to put a foot down to a pedal and skip onto the saddle of my newly adopted bike, Paddy to do the foot switcheroo and complete the skip-on to what had started the whole thing as my bike. All done within the freewheeling half-mile or so of Belmont Avenue, Donnybrook, by two foolhardy sixteen-year-olds in the year of the Lord 1943.

———

We had been through the drill several times and it was at the end of a full performance that the condition of the permanent way put a sudden end to the 'yippee' with which we were celebrating our success.

Paddy's front mudguard, I remember, was black and heavy, in section like a capital C with the ends turned in into tiny tight tubes along the edges, intended to give rigidity. Unfortunately a crack in this rigid edge had quickly spread across and made that mudguard very fragile indeed. The road surfaces were in a pretty desperate state of neglect, potholes abounded, and the tall thin wheel of a bike is much more liable to dislocation from such obstacles than the fat squat wheel of your well-sprung modern car. Anyway, my front wheel (that is, the one on Paddy's bike of course) hit a nasty pothole in the otherwise smooth follow-through to the Great Bicycle Exchange which we had just executed, the jolt jackknifed the front mudguard around its sensitive fissure, the lower end of the mudguard slammed and jammed up into the top of the front fork, and jerked the bike to a very sudden stop. I executed the classic vault over the handlebars and landed headfirst on the road in front with a fearful ringing bang on my skull.

---

All perfectly clear, but I haven't got the faintest idea what happened next. Some time later, perhaps a couple of minutes, perhaps only a few seconds, I was sitting on the road in front of a slightly twisted bike, I had a pain in my head, and I did not know what had happened between the head-bang and the sitting. There was of course no real harm done, traffic was nil, a sixteen-year-old's skull is very hard, and there was no part of a bicycle we couldn't repair in minutes.

I have always resented that gap in my private personal history. I have tried to console myself by telling myself that probably not much happened anyway in those few seconds, or at most minutes. Vast stretches of my life, totaling days, weeks, months, have been allowed to slip into the same opacity. But I did know, during the intervals which made up those days and weeks, what was happening, while it was happening, and so to speak voluntarily relinquished my knowledge of it when I decided it was not worth keeping. With that bang on the head on Belmont Avenue I got no options.

---

It is one thing to have no past, or to have no memory to account for some part of it; it is quite another to have no future. Paddy, who had shared with me those glorious days of the bicycle, was dying of an incurable malignancy, a tumour, cancer, damn it. He knew it, I knew it, each of us knew the other knew it. He told me about it himself, with fascinating clinical detail on how the cancer would progress. When I left him, after hearing this bitter news, my mind was flooded with the enormity of a vanishing future and I could understand it only in terms of my lost few seconds of vanished past on Belmont Avenue.

When I left him, I had to decide so many things—which route would I take homeward, did I need petrol, would my wife want the car that afternoon? Each moment I was manufacturing my own future and he was lying there with none, or at best an ever-contracting one.

I called to see him frequently and he chatted as brightly as ever about our mutual interests, sport, public affairs, the careers of friends. I listened carefully, almost counting his words, to see if he would reveal a shift in his perspective, an abandonment of the trivial forward-planning which I had suddenly learnt filled almost the whole of my life. There was no such revelation.

———

I was convinced that someone situated as he was must turn away from the shrinking future to the substantial past and I decided that yes indeed I would count the words. First the past-loaded words—*was, used to, old days, remember, ago, what happened to*—then the future-loaded words—*going to, hope, expect, plan, intend, will, look out for, tomorrow, next*. And I would compare his past–future ratio with that of a normal subject.

In practice that survey proved quite tricky. The secret agent's bug for recording purposes was beyond my resources and an openly carried tape recorder in a condemned cell would have macabre memorial qualities. Manual methods, however covert the intention, would also excite comment. An ostentatious rosary beads in each hand (left for past, right for future) would be an admirable counting aid for numbers up to fifty-nine each but would imply an unwonted devotion to pious practices and carry similarly macabre overtones.

Eventually I did it on my eight three-jointed fingers and my two two-jointed thumbs—each joint is either a one or a nought—and tabulated the results:

per 1000 words

|                | past words | future words |
|----------------|------------|--------------|
| terminal case  | 21.34      | 22.08        |
| normal subject | 22.63      | 20.98        |

The differences, you might think, are statistically insignificant but they lie in the unexpected direction. My dying friend was thinking more of the future than was his normal peer. And let me emphasise that this was no reflection of a preoccupation on his part with the hereafter. References to the spiritual aspects of his situation were confined to the remark now and then that a priest friend had called or would be calling to see him and I could presume therefore that he had put that side of his affairs in order to his own satisfaction.

It became necessary for me to analyse in a qualitative way, rather than merely quantitatively, the content of what he was saying. And it proved to show a considerable concern with those very planning segments of living which I had thought would sink into insignificance. As the allotted span grew shorter, he grew more and more engrossed with the remaining months, weeks, and days.

———

'Dr. Ryan will be in tomorrow and he asked me about that hi-fi layout there. Would you ever go to the reference library and look up the back-file of *Practical Electronics*? I think it was June about three years ago, it had to be early summer anyway because I spent the whole summer putting the bloody thing together and it's certainly more than two years ago, would you ever get me a photocopy of the article and the circuits, I'll have to show it to him.'

———

There had been, I must confess, a selfish part in the motivation for my visits to my friend. It was he who had been with me on that morning on Belmont Avenue when I had mislaid part of my personal history and I had hoped that he would dwell more and more on the past and at some point perhaps recall my missing experience. Obviously I wasn't going to jog him in any particular direction but there was no harm in hoping. His increasing concentration on the future made me abandon what little expectation I had had.

———

'Melon seeds,' he said, 'fastest-growing thing you ever saw. We had melon at our dinner the other week and one of the nurses got me an empty margarine tub and a few spoonfuls of clay and turf-mould, would you look at them? Of course they'll have to be planted out in a while and get plenty of moisture. I always thought they grew in swamps beside the Mississippi but if we're lucky we may get a few viable plants out of that lot.'

Again: 'I see the old bike is making a comeback with the price of oil and all this environmental awareness. There's an old crock in the shed at home and a couple of hours' work should get it going. All it needs is a bit of a cleanup and lashin's of oil. 'S'pose a three-speed'd make it more useful for the middle-aged.'

'Great gas, mending bikes,' I contributed. 'We should revive the lost arts. There must be very few of us left who can line a bald tyre with another bald tyre with the wire rim ripped off it.'

'Did you ever use the sticky goo off a burning lump of old tyre as an adhesive for sticking on patches? God, what a mess. But it worked, for a while anyway.'

———

He never mentioned any advance or delay that may have been suggested by his doctors in his estimated time of departure but as the time yet to run became obviously shorter there was if anything an intensification in his commitment to forward-planning.

'Of course you can see I'm not as mobile as I'd like but it just gave me a great idea for typing. We must get onto IBM or somebody, it'd be great PR for them to get into the handicapped racket. Look, just one hand, five fingers. You set up a keyboard that your fingertips sit comfortably on, now the combination of five fingers taken one, two, three, four, or five at a time gives you thirty-one positions, that has to be enough for all the letters of the alphabet, full stop, comma, line space and shift, and the shift will give you a few more punctuation marks.'

I must have withdrawn somewhat in my amazement at this fresh outburst of his forward-thinking, for he stared at me briefly. 'Hey,' he broke in, 'are you still there? You look as if you were miles away. You know what you remind me of? D'you remember the day you knocked yourself out on Belmont Avenue when you were thrown over the handlebars? You sat there like an eejit for about ten seconds before you got up and you were staring at me with your eyes open but it was perfectly clear you weren't seeing me; that's what you were like just now. But anyway do you know anybody in the stationery business that could work up that typewriter idea? Of course how would the bloody typewriter know that little finger and thumb, say, weren't separate signals, nobody would ever get them dead synchronised; no I've got it, you set up the signal with the fingers and then you give an execute command like this look by slapping down with your wrist.' He laid his hand, very thin now, on the fold-down of his white sheet and drummed gently with his fingertips, then slapped his wrist-joint up and down a few times.

———

I never thought of death, really; living was stretching before me forever, freewheeling from a faraway Sandford to an ever-receding Donnybrook. Paddy's future was contracting at an ever-accelerating rate, piling back at him, building up a vast tidal bore, rushing into an ever-narrowing creek to engulf him suddenly in one great catastrophic moment when the sudden-ending past would slam and jam against the sudden-stopping future.

———

'God,' he exclaimed, 'were you ever in a canoe caught in surf? The waves are rushing in toward the shore and as it gets shallower the bottom of the water is scraped harder and harder on the sand or whatever down below, braked harder and harder by it, the tops of the waves are free-flowing and won't be retarded, they press on and curl over, if you're in a light boat and get caught on top of one of them you're grabbed by the twirling wave-top and you start to shoot forward as if you'd been given an engine and you know all the time it's because the water down below is being braked, pushed back, well, I'm like that now, everything is pushed back against me and I'm being whirled forward, I'm moving through so much so quickly and everything is

## Swopping Names

I'm no good at describing faces so's you'd recognise them (and neither is anybody else for that matter) but this face I would recognise again anywhere though I am absolutely certain I had never seen it before, so I'd better have a go at describing it.

On a sunny Saturday morning Shop Street in Galway is pretty crowded, path and roadway almost a pedestrian precinct without benefit of corporation bye-law. I was just leaving O'Gorman's bookshop and stood back for a moment in the wide porch before pushing into the crowd. Two young women, talking animatedly together, were among those passing and one of them suddenly looked up, caught my eye, smiled, waved a greeting, and called me by my name. She had pale skin and very dark hair, kept fairly short, with a slight wave, high cheekbones, grey eyes, very little makeup. About early to mid twenties in age and overall fairly pretty. I know, I swear, I mean I know with absolute certainty that I had never seen her before. She and her companion quickly passed and disappeared in the passing throng.

How did she know my name?

I had not been living long in this city and, small as it is, I have not so many circles of acquaintance that a handsome woman, many years my junior, could be familiar enough to call my name in greeting and nevertheless disappear entirely into the formless background of a bad memory. But I am long enough here for that girl to have been only a kid when I left Dublin, so there is no possibility that she's someone out of a past acquaintanceship.

The uncomfortable feeling arises that she and I have met in some part of my existence of which I am now completely unaware or of which I am always unconscious. Where that part took place, or when, I cannot imagine. I am not subject to blackouts, I have never gone off on long alcoholic and dirty lost weekends. In fact (I know this sounds corny but I'm driven to it) the only part of my life remaining unaccounted for and in the course of which I might have known this girl is the one third of my life I have spent asleep.

That anything of lasting importance should happen during sleep is ridiculous, in the view of naive materialists, who think of us as lumps of matter inhabited (while awake!) by a switch-on switch-off spirit, mind, soul, brain, or some such thing. A more complicated and less materialistic view can, however, be proposed, suggesting that the spirit, mind, soul, et cetera, is always present and correct, sir, able and willing to work but unable to find work—because the very limited lump of matter which it uses as its workstation has had to be withdrawn from service for repair and refurbishment, recharging of batteries, or, if you like, sleep.

Dreams have had a rotten press because so many stupid and spurious claims have been made about them. They are so trivial that only reinforcement gives them a glimmer of survival. So I've dreamt about an electric tram, let's say, some fragment of my lost youth and I've completely forgotten the dream-image. I wake, get up, go to work, and in the course of the day I happen to come across an old picture of an electric tram. 'Gosh, I had a dream about one of those last night!' This is a commonplace experience and needs only the slightest shift to make it look as if dreams are prophetic. 'Dream about a tramcar at night and you'll see one the next day.' No account taken of course of the millions of things I dream about which are not recalled and reinforced by coincidental random encounter and so sink without a trace.

Now my seeing that girl in Shop Street and being seen by her certainly did not make me exclaim 'Gosh, I dreamt about a girl just like that last night!' but she could, without my remembering it, have been in my dreams, or I in hers, or, let's say, in sleep-time experience.

Hereabouts, in the city, very few people would greet me who are not friends or acquaintances but I don't have to go far from the city to be in places where most people would greet though few if any know me. It will vary from the finger raised from the steering wheel as a greeting between passing motorists, to the friendly wave of a passing cyclist, to brief spoken words of passing pedestrians. The smaller the community, the more so.

Take Rathlin, a strange island halfway between Ireland and Scotland, neither the one thing nor the other. It is a mixture of basalt and chalk. Cliffs crumbled onto beaches below make speckled plains of black basalt and white chalk. In massive boulders of soft chalky limestone are round nodules of hard glassy flint. There are only about thirty households on the island, maybe a hundred people. None of them know me but all of them greet me, smiling, saluting, waving. Perhaps they are welcoming me to their nightside existence, where I am on short leave from another place.

I scrambled along that patchwork foreshore to reach the white chalk cliffs. I passed thousands of rocks of all shapes and sizes, then perhaps a shattered, weathered, wicker lobster-pot, long abandoned by fishermen and tossed here by the sea. Then a coil of blue nylon rope lying tangled on a mat of seaweed. Each of these undistinguished features made little impression on me and was immediately forgotten. Or almost so. On my return scramble, an hour later, as I saw the pot or the rope or a rusty oil drum the memory clicked and I registered the fact that yes, I had seen that on my outward way. Just as the dream-image is recalled by an old photograph of an electric tram.

I was lying on the rocky beach, curled snugly on a mat of seaweed, against a small, smooth boulder. Just in from a long swim, I was luxuriously coiled against the warm rounded rock-surface, my own curves languorously intertwined.

The mysticals, for whom I haven't much time, would say that we can sense when we are being stared at. 'I stared at him so hard he looked up,' or 'I felt that someone was staring at me and glanced up quickly and there he was,' that kind of thing. Total baloney if you ask me. They never say what sense it is that does this 'feeling.' I suppose the well-packed portmanteau of the sixth of the series. Personally I rely on the others. A new sound or a cessation of a slight continuous sound would be enough, a faint shadow moving or coming to rest, out of focus, at the limit of peripheral vision. That day it was probably the scrunch-scrunch of feet scrambling over the rocky foreshore. I had heard it once, uninterrupted, on the rim of sensation. Now, an hour or so later, I heard it again and only then recalled the earlier hearing. Now it was interrupted by the slightest pause. And there he was staring at me. Mercifully he didn't come over to kick or tug me from my bed as I feared for a tense moment he might.

On the main island, in the city of Galway, I was walking along Shop Street one day, just passing the bookshop, when I glanced up and saw this middle-aged, for God's sake elderly guy in the entrance. When our eyes met, he suddenly smiled and waved and greeted me by name. This was no pick-up or try-on; he didn't make a move to come forward out of the porch, to get into or through the crowds strolling by. The funny thing is, I could swear I'd never seen him before in my whole life, so how on earth did he know my name?

## Space Invaders

I once bought a bubble can, a small canister of thick soapy fluid, which came with a short plastic rod having an open ring at one end an inch or so across. I dipped the ringed end into the canister and when I took it out the ring was filled with a thin film of the fluid. I blew on this film and it expanded rapidly and sailed from the ring in a long series of small iridescent bubbles. With practice, I learnt to blow more gently and to produce not a series of bubbles but one large one, which floated downward, though slowly, nevertheless behaving like a body endowed with noticeable weight and mass. It was surprisingly robust and could bump against other objects and, provided they were not too sharp-edged, bounce off without bursting. When it had sunk to the floor it sat quietly oscillating for a while, the fibres of the carpet indenting its surface, the indentations visible to me, above, through its transparent skin. The skin began to disappear and become invisible in expanding blotches of vacancy before the whole thing ceased to exist.

I used to think that I live inside some such bubble, inside a skin coterminous with my outermost dermis, that this bubble-skin is the frontier between me and the rest, that there is nothing within it but my vacant self-consciousness, that when that finest skin would become eroded and blotched, would evaporate, I would be dead; but that is too special, too self-centred a theory. If I am in a bubble, each of the others must be in one as well. I must brood further on experience to work out a more generous and a more general theory.

———

A small table in a small restaurant on a busy summer weekend is the place where bubble encounters are most likely to be experienced. OK, so they're my friends, mates, colleagues, comrades. We didn't mind how close together we sat (we thought), but it was a few years since we'd been at school together, slapping one another's shoulders, pushing and shoving bodies, no respecters of persons or their places. That kind of thing would have been a bit queer or a bit free once puberty had established itself fully over the emerging adults. I sat down carefully between spreading thighs to left and right, which spread only just that far. I stirred my coffee, the elbow carefully avoiding giving offence or puncture to left or right. But the nearer the radii get to the centre of the circle the closer they come together. Thus with the knees and feet under the table. Even with skins of stocking and leather, the shoe is an assailant. 'Oh, sorry, we're a bit crowded,' on the darting touch and go of toe or ankle, let's say, or chance touch of knee to knee. A waitress came with a tray of drinks, leant between us to reach the table. Perilously close, the bubbles pendulously touching. She was big-bosomed, tight-waisted in her white-trimmed costume, wide-skirted. As she leant over, I could see that one of the packed young men across the table was glancing into the gape at the bosom of her dress. His hand moved and I would have screamed but of course it was nothing so gross, we were civilised people. She laid on the table, after the tray, a card with our bill on it and his hand, with a five-pound note, flashed out in time to touch hers. Only a gasp then, not a scream, but her bubble was all around her hand too and he had punctured it, a crude sacrilege.

———

'Bonjour,' each said in succession to the other, 'bonjour, bonjour.' Each arrival in the office greeted each of the others with a gentle handshake. I recalled all the folklore: hand to hand is safer than hand to sword-hilt and a guarantee of peace, or they are all Freemasons, giving a secret sign. It is another secret, a secret permitted entrance through the bubble, a hissing puncture.

———

Moon rocks (they said) might be infested with horrid micro-organisms, the sperm or spawn of little green men, I suppose, which could have increased and multiplied in earth's cozy atmosphere and taken us over or exterminated us. When Jim Irwin came back from the moon with his mates, they and their clothes and their craft were all grotty with the dust off the clumsy rocks they were lugging about. Of course they had dumped their expedition trash bags, including excrement bags, on the unfortunate moon, so I suppose it's only fair. Anyway the show must go on, so when we saw pictures of the scientists handling these dangerous articles they were taking oh so special precautions. The rock was in a glass box; into holes in the sides of the box were set small portholes fitted with flexible inward-pointing gloves, so the scientist could shove his hands into the gloves and freely manipulate the fragment of moon without any skin contact.

So monstrously premature babies might be handled or cultures of deadly microbes.

———

*Amnion*; the word rolled sonorously round in my head, its humming nasals sounding like a name from Greek drama. This was the innermost membrane surrounding the unborn within me. The amniotic sac burst with a flood of waters, the spasms (sweat, pain) squeeeeeezed out the head. I don't remember much more until they gave me the warm moist squeezed little lamb to hold against my body, my warm moist breast. 'Look here,' the nurse said, proffering a hand's span of gauzy film, 'she's a lucky baby, she was born with a caul.'

She will never drown in flooding waters, storm demons will not torment her, she will see and speak with spirits, this token of her life will stay firm and taut and she will be in good health. This fragment of her earthly bubble will be her genius, to direct her.

Already she has cried once, in fear, thrill, and surprise at this other world outside.

———

I was sitting isolated in my car one dark evening, waiting at a busy crossing for a traffic light to change. I was in the inside lane, ready to go straight ahead. Beside me were the cars in the outside lane, waiting to turn off. My eyes were fixed on the light in front but with peripheral vision I suddenly saw the mass of a car rushing toward us from the side. It should have been making a tight right-angle turn but was moving much too fast, swinging too far out, and I knew for a perceptible interval before it happened that happen it must: the lurching car smashed into the front of one of those lined up beside me. Perception slowed then and the blurred crash was followed by a thin stream, an arc of twinkling glass fragments dancing prettily in headlamp beams, tinkling to the ground.

I switched off my engine and got out, walking nervously the couple of yards to full view of the accident. I saw the shattered windscreen, what was left of it crazed with a gauze of fine white cracks. A head was sticking through it, face-down, pouring blood onto the bonnet. I could not tell if it was a man or a woman. It was probably dead.

———

'Keep away from children' the notice said. I knew it wasn't an injunction to me to avoid youngsters but rather a caution against letting the plastic bag on which the notice was written pass into dangerous hands. I wondered was it really so dangerous and stuck my head into it, drawing, or trying to draw, a deep breath. The bag contracted suddenly and stickily against the skin of my face and head, slapping against lips, eyes, ears, and specially nose. The inflow of breath stopped with the sudden jerk of the adhering membrane. I puffed outward and my exhausted air refilled the bag, bellying it out. Relief was my instantaneous thought but the puff had to be followed by a gulp of inhalation and again the film flapped like a valve, sealing my nostrils. Enough; one more puff outward to release it and I tore the thing from my head, the relief this time genuine and fulfilled.

———

'I see,' the doctor said, 'I see, I see. Well we better have a look, it's probably nothing at all to worry about, lots of conditions would explain it, probably no need to worry at all, if you'd just slip up on the couch please and loosen your clothing.' He turned away discreetly, with his left hand pushing a small wheeled screen between us, dropping on his desk from his right hand the large index card with my particulars. As he stepped to the washstand basin I slipped off my panties and reclined on the couch, lifting my skirt. He worked the taps at the basin with his elbows, pressing elongated handles left and right, hot and cold, lathering under the one, rinsing under the other. He took from a wall-mounted packet by the basin a pair of gloves made of the finest polythene film. He slipped his hands into the gloves and turned back. Coming past the screen, he looked down at my panties on the chair beside the couch, took up the absorbent pad I had been wearing in the panties, looked closely at it, and sniffed at it. 'I'll give you a clean pad,' he said, lifting with a tread of his foot the lid of a gleaming enamel disposal bin and dropping the pad within. 'Let's have a look now, OK? Turn on your side, please.' He leant over me peering and sniffing. Then the cold fingers of his filmy gloves touched me. I braced slightly as I felt the cold plastic inside me. 'OK, OK,' he said. He wiped gently on the inside surface with a small swab. 'OK, that's all.' He turned away, facing the desk, held the swab close to his face, then disposed of it and the plastic gloves in the enamel bin.

I stood up, pulled on my panties, dropped and smoothed my skirt. 'Perfectly normal discharge, there's mucous membranes all over the body more or less producing their own lubrication, nothing at all to worry about, no growths if that's what was worrying you, just keep up careful hygiene.'

———

When I am old, a knock will come to the door and I will shuffle up the narrow hall. I will carefully place the knob of the safety chain, hanging on the doorjamb, in the short slot fastened to the door. I will open the door, to the six-inch limit of the lengthened and stiffened chain, my bubble steel-reinforced. 'Would the lady want any carpets or lino?' the strong rough young man will say, a grin on his red face, suntanned below his sun-bleached reddish hair. 'No, thank you.' 'I've the best of stuff here mam, straight from the factory, the best of prices.' His eyes will drop—to my legs? no—to the worn patch of lino just inside the hall door. 'No thank you.' He will turn quickly and walk away.

---

Sitting opposite me after dinner one evening, he opened his mouth wide, stuck a finger into it, jabbed the finger at something, and swallowed. I stared in disgust. 'Sorry,' he said, 'the soup was so bloody hot it raised a blister on the roof of my mouth, always seem huge to the touch of your tongue but it's such a thin layer it heals very fast so the only thing is to burst it.' What abuse he might inflict on himself in the cold dark of his bed I did not care but here before my eyes was his personal puncturing of his personal bubble, a self-inflicted wound, flagrant and ostentatious masturbation, the finger entering one of his own private orifices, his bubble a self-destroying shape, an unbeholdable Möbius bottle.

---

We embraced once more and his closeness excited me. I lost my head and then God help us my maidenhead. Although he penetrated me, in a phrase for which there is no elegant alternative, my bubble was not ruptured, nor was his. It was as though we were isolated by a double film stretched over our intimate parts, more subtle but more real than Gossamer, or Magic Touch, or Intime, or Stopes's Delicatesse, or whatever other name the rubber companies might dream up for their preservatives.

———

I must get back to the bubbles. When I blew them from the little ring they were full and round, yielding conventional curved reflections of windows and other highlights. But as they died they blanked out in irregular patches. A spreading area would just cease to reflect, become a black hole, thin beyond the thinnest of thin-film physics, a black but transparent hole, reflecting nothing. And this while some parts of the bubble's globe remained sound, a rounded and still reflective surface, gleaming with swirling wave-forms of red, orange, yellow, and so on.

When I am old I shall go again to a cathedral in France where there is a maze in a pattern of tiles on the floor. I wandered, just a tourist, strolling around with the crowd. As we passed behind the high altar I noticed in a quiet side chapel a small congregation hearing Mass. I knelt with them and listened to the flowing French of the celebrant. It was the early days of the vernacular liturgy and his speech, in psalm or prayer or preaching, was exotic and bewitching. After the consecration he passed amongst us, shaking hands, as we did with one another, murmuring gentle words of peace, in my case haltingly spoken. After the blessing we filed out of the chapel, joining again the other tourists ambling through the cathedral.

Suddenly we were dappled with swirling patches, suffused waves of red, green, and blue, intermittently bright or dull or fading to the uniform pale grey of the limestone floor. I looked up and became aware of two things simultaneously, first that it was noon and a high sun, occasionally obscured by cloud, was shining on the south transept's great window, beneath which we stood, and also that all these peaceful people were with me inside a glorious shimmering aureole.

Harsh white lights switched on near us, beams picking out details otherwise camouflaged in dim heights above us—the clustered, fluted pipes of a great organ and a musicians' gallery near the roof. An organ and trumpet concert for national television was being rehearsed. The throb of deep wooden pipes heterodyned with the high metal purity of the trumpet, the whole fabric of the ancient building vibrated with the interfering oscillations. Throaty bourdon and bombarde died away and the tight reed of the trumpeter's lips sang on alone, a sustained angelic voice, pure and clean.

With a shivering tinkle a panel of coloured glass shattered and fell from the window; a beam of natural white light from the sun poured in upon me. A couple of other tinkles followed, coloured patches of the window-bubble blotched out piecemeal. There were urgent shouts, the music stopped, the priest who had just finished Mass rushed out of the dark behind the high altar, volubly ushering out the amazed tourists.

We walked out into the crowded street, glistening with a new illumination.

A
NARRATIVE
of the
PROCEEDINGS
of the
BOUNTY OF NATURE ENTERPRISE
on its
VOYAGE IN SEARCH OF THE FRUIT TREE,

in which are incorporated
portions of the
JOURNAL
written by her Captain;


A NEW EDITION
to which is added
AN APPENDIX,
based upon the log of the hunting vessel
*Charles Morgan* of New Bedford, Israel Hands, Master.


MMXXXVIII

CHRISTIAN, FLETCHER (18th cent.) British seaman, the ringleader in the mutiny of the *Bounty,* which sailed to Tahiti in 1787-88. In 1808 his descendants were found on Pitcairn Island.

PITCAIRN ISLANDS Pop. (1983) 61; area 27 sq km. Island group in the SE Pacific Ocean, E of French Polynesia; chief settlement, Adamstown; volcanic islands, with high lava cliffs and rugged hills; equable climate; occupied by nine mutineers from HMS *Bounty,* 1790.

—*Encyclopaedia Universalis*
(22nd ed.)

EPISTLE DEDICATORY
to the
President and Council
of the
ROYAL SOCIETY

MADAM,

One already honoured by your learned and venerable Council when entrusted with the preparation of a narrative recounting the melancholy events attending the voyage of the *Bounty of Nature Enterprise* to a remote planet must feel himself doubly so when afforded the facility, in the compilation of that narrative, of consulting the precious records confided to the keeping of your Council by the commander of that Enterprise on his return from the arduous expedition of which the following pages bear an inadequate chronicle, written by the hand of one who will thereafter be ever sensible of those honours and will remain

Ever your dutiful and humble servant

ALF MAC LOCHLAINN

# A Narrative &c., &c.

The family of Bligh, from which descended the person central to the ensuing narrative, was of sturdy yeoman stock in the northwest country and in earlier centuries, enjoying the patronage of the local landed gentry, had given many of its sons to the middle levels of the Army, the Navy, and the Church. It had also given to many of its sons the Christian name William.

One William, father of the William of whom we will mainly treat, took to wife a lady of the family of Christian, of the Isle of Man, where persons of that surname are numerous. He had a distinguished career in the public service under the late Queen and in 1988, dubbed by wits in the public prints (in honour of the tercentenary then being celebrated) the Year of the Inglorious Counter-Revolution, was responsible for the acquisition by the Government of the United Kingdom, from the Soviet Union, then crumbling under certain effects of that counter-revolution, of several items of cosmonautical equipment found surplus to the requirements of that unhappy land. These included unmotored bodies and frames of vehicles of various sizes originally destined for the exploration of Deep Space.

The said William and his lady became the parents of a son William, our subject, whom the name William will alone denote hereafter. The boy was early accustomed to the ways of the sea, spending happy days in the summer on smaller fishing smacks out of

Fleetwood and Whitehaven and learning in his child-
ish way to 'box the compass' as the old salts taught
him.

Approaching the years of young manhood, William
proved a youth of likely parts and was sent for better
instruction to a College of Technology, where he
quickly mastered subjects of interest and utility (as
Physics, Newtonian, modern, and cosmic; Biology,
including genetic engineering; Chronometry; Mathematics, including conic sections, curve dynamics with
ballistics and trajectories; Navigation, terrestrial,
celestial, and cosmonautical), adding these to such
practical skills as the boy sailor had already learnt.

During the extended summer vacations allowed to
students in higher education, the young and athletic
William continued to enjoy his sailing, taking part in
competitive events which took him south-about round
the island of Ireland and thence on an exhilarating
roller-coaster through the Western Isles and a rush
into the North Channel and to the Isle of Man and
home to Fleetwood or Whitehaven; and in ocean-sailing
cruises north, south, east, and west.

Admitted to more advanced studies, he satisfied his
professors with a dissertation on *The Dynamics of an
Asteroid,* and secured an appointment as Navigation
Officer on a Deep Space probe utilising the Soviet ship
bodies above alluded to, now fitted with Double-A
motors, assembled in Near Space orbit into large complex units and equipped with twin shuttles, the one for
ferrying crew and supplies between Earth bases and
the Complex in orbit and between the Complex and
such other heavenly bodies as chance or planning
might place in its path; the other as a system in reserve
to ensure the safety of the members of the crew should
the main craft or the first shuttle develop faults *en
route* beyond the powers of the crew to make good.

The Complex was under the command of a skilful if strict master, one Capt. Cook, and there began a series of shakedown cruises in low orbit and then in Near Space, in the course of which the heretofore experimental vessels were deemed to have proven fit for extended voyages; and William and the other young cadets, under the able tutelage of Capt. Cook, mastered further practical skills exemplifying the application of theoretical principles with which they had earlier been made familiar in the study. Capt. Cook, however, advised his young charges that they might conveniently forget for the present much of the instruction they had received in their academies and concentrate their attention instead on two fundamental practical and aesthetic considerations: *primo,* a spacecraft, however powerful and ingenious its propulsion, is not driven—after its launch if that launch be perfect—rather it sails; and *secundo,* the curvilinear routes along which it travels are of surpassing elegance.

The faint windlike forces guiding the craft, he would explain, are as the faint caresses at the remotest end of ripples from a great fan, the 'fan' or source of power being, initially, the moon and sun, thereafter other heavenly bodies, whose gravitational fields exert attractions, now great, now small, upon the tiny globule of metal and plastic placed by its human pilots on invisible trackways across the firmament. The concatenation of these attractions generates complex curving courses throughout Deep Space, bearing the frail humans sinuously to their destinations. The Captain demonstrated by touching the screen before him on the control panel and evoking an image of these knitted trackways, then enlarging them so that each particular curve swelled and arched in microscopic detail, each bend swervingly bending more and more under unseen signals, the distant beckonings of many stars to right

or left or up or down, all direction meaningless save
the one predetermined course that always lay ahead,
'through the calm firmament' (as Cook pointed out the
poet had written), 'but up or down, by center or ec-
centric hard to tell, in numbers that compute days,
months, and years, they turn their various motions or
are turned by the magnetic beam that, though unseen,
shoots invisible virtue even to the Deep.'

Young William Bligh had charge, early in these
cruises, of the application to propulsion of the Double-
A motors of the Complex, dubbed Double-A in the free
speech of the cosmonauts as being designed to operate
at two levels, the one atomic, the other sub-atomic and
being, in fine, based on two simple principles, namely,
that the fractions of subdivided fundamental particles
when released from their intimate bonding with their
nuclei escape with a velocity almost equal to that of
light; and further, that action and reaction being equal
and opposite, the emission of a stream of such fundamental particles from such a body as the Complex, of
the order of magnitude, in relation to the infinity of
Deep Space, of a non-gravitational free weightless
particle, must generate motion in that Complex at a
speed approaching that of light itself. The first or
Single-A motor was applied only for manoeuvres of
the craft in Near Space prior to launch proper.

A second cruise took the Complex to a galaxy known
to earthbound astronomers as T.1014, numbered thus
within an area known as Titan. The Captain had
decided that the title of his exalted patron, the Royal
Society, for which he was carrying out extensive cosmo-
graphical enquiries, might be used in any more precise
delineation of heavenly bodies to be encountered in
close passes to Titan and took it upon himself to de-
nominate a particular group of stars in the area the
Society Cluster.

A final close pass about the cluster was followed by
an entry into its system, selection of a single star and
examination of that star's satellite planets. To one of
these in particular Cook directed his attention, circling
it in low orbit. He then dispatched a shuttle for even
closer examination of his chosen objective. The shuttle,
too, circled the planet in low orbit, then skimmed on
the thick upper layer of its atmosphere, entered it and
burnt a quick way through it, glided over seas and
land, blue and green as at home, splashed down and
floated to a safe landfall beside the welcoming shore
of a calm lagoon. Activated by this landing, sensors
deployed and quickly advised of a safe external environment and the crew walked safely, a little unsteadily
but heavy-footed as at home, on firm ground spread
with grass and flowers.

Thus walking for a short space, they soon encountered beings, like themselves in being 'hairless upright
bipeds,' but unlike them in many other respects. That
they were male and female as on Earth was manifest,
as they wore no clothing. The balmy air did not require
it for warmth and the male and female organs freely
displayed betokened a lack of those restraints which
obtained in earthbound humankind. The skin, so laid
bare, was covered in what the visitors first deemed
ornamental whorls of coloured paints but which they
learned later were designs as 'twere engraved on their
skin by many prickings and the rubbing-in of coloured
substances from the soil and from vegetable matter.

These people, for nothing else could they be considered, met them smiling and offering food and drink,
bread and sweet fruit juices, which refreshed and
enlivened the bodies and minds long used to the pro-
cessed pastes of voyage fare.

Our cosmonauts were filled with curiosity as to who
these people might be and whence they came, but

before posing such questions to their kindly hosts,
as they quickly proved themselves to be by their signs
of friendship, must needs devote themselves to a learning of their language. They spoke mellifluously, with
vowels as known to many of the peoples of Earth, liquid
and nasal consonants, few plosives and a resistance to
diphthongs, uttering words which seemed tuneful
enough to the visitors, as *kalanuri, akatea, nurangi-
nurangi.* From names for foods and drinks, the visitors
quickly progressed to names for persons. 'Cook' the
natives of the planet could enunciate without difficulty, though with 'Bligh' they encountered a stum-
bling block, as they frequently confused those sounds
which writers of English represent with the letters
*r* and *l*, and split diphthongs into their constituent
vowels; our William, therefore, became known to them
as 'Berahee.' And some of the visitors fell into un-
seemly laughter to hear the natives later confuse
'regal' and 'legal,' 'light' and 'right,' 'long' and 'wrong.'
The natives appeared to have no name for their own
place and learned to use the name given to them by
their visitors, sadly misformed, 'Titan' with its intrac-
table diphthong becoming 'Taheetan.'

The friendships quickly progressed to such end that
the women of the place soon invited the visiting men,
by movements held lascivious on Earth, to share their
beds. This communication by signs was, however, soon
followed by an ability to speak the language and Capt.
Cook learned that the people of the place understood
their forefathers had always been there, that they had
been placed there by a powerful being who dwelt in the
sky and who had made for them the green grass and
the fruitful trees, the mountains, plains and valleys,
the white beaches, the rocky reefs and the sea, and all
the animals of water and land. Seeing it so beautiful,
the powerful being had decided that it might be shared

with others somewhat though not entirely in its own likeness and had set upon the ground the ancestors of those now speaking to visiting people who had come in flames from the great blue vault of the sky. They enjoyed all the beauties of the land in equality, knew no bound of 'mine' or 'thine' in property of persons or things, save in a mild privacy of intimate relations in their simple round houses built of wood and straw.

The great power had given them, for their principal sustenance, a Tree, which, growing to forty metres in height, was decked in due season with dark green, glossy, many-lobed leaves, then bright yellow flowers, and then large berries or nuts. The pith of these nuts (in reality ripened ovaries, as the biologist Bligh was able to determine) the people would crumble and bake as with our bread, or would slice it and cook it into delicious wafers of sweetmeat.

Capt. Cook, ever mindful of his duty to the most prestigious of his patrons, realised that the council of the Royal Society must find the discovery of such a valuable food plant of the highest interest and determined that specimens of it should be garnered for return to Earth. Accordingly he instructed William Bligh to climb a stately specimen of the Tree and harvest some of its fruits. Obedient to his orders, young Bligh mounted the trunk of the tree into its lower branches, scrabbled among the foliage, and chopped off a number of burgeoning new shoots, which he dropped to his Captain below. Suddenly Bligh, hidden in the branches, grew still in fear as he heard a great hubbub break out. Numbers of the people of the place, men and women, had gathered around about Capt. Cook and were abusing him in loud voices while they threatened him with the heavy stones and thick boughs they carried in their hands. Bligh understood enough of their language to comprehend that they were bitterly complaining that Cook had in hand a business permitted only to the King and Queen, as might be, who alone had the right to take the first sproutings from a new-budded springtime tree such as, at that very moment, hid in its lower branches the frightened young cadet.

Hoping no worse might befall, Bligh was all the more horrified when he saw the press of bodies draw aside to allow passage of a more stately figure, garbed in a shimmering cloak of bright feathers and armed with a heavy sword, with which he imperiously struck at the unfortunate Capt. Cook, who fell dead upon the ground with great effusion of blood.

William Bligh could never recall exactly how long he had spent hiding in the tree, but when some unstated time had elapsed after the departure of the angry natives, he stealthily climbed down and, as stealthily skirting the bloody remains of his late commander, made his way to the shuttle, nestling safely in a snug cove. He quickly established communication with the ship-keeper, orbiting in the Complex, and arranged an urgent shuttle-launch, and a rendezvous and docking in Near Space.

Securely docked, Bligh, now, by default, in charge of the Complex, had little time to contemplate the awfulness of his situation. Deprived of the guidance and counsel of a beloved superior, he had to marshal all his practical and theoretical skills to plot thrust-power, gravitational fields, and chronometry for a melancholy return journey to Earth and he reflected sombrely, if briefly, on his youthful disquisition on the dynamics of an asteroid as he made these preparations to inject himself and his remaining companions into a course cruising through the heavens toward home. On the journey, he resolved to exercise one further pre-rogative of a commander in choosing a designation for the beautiful but fearsome place on a planet in the Society Cluster where Cook had met his end, and named it Assassination Cove.

The skill, judgement, and maturity he had shown in accomplishing the safe return to Earth of the Complex were duly rewarded but after some years in relatively unexciting occupation about the business of the Astronautical Fleet he was gratified to be the recipient of the following letter.

## 𝕽𝖔𝖞𝖆𝖑 𝕾𝖔𝖈𝖎𝖊𝖙𝖞

Lt. Wm. Bligh, A.F.

Sir,

I am to communicate to you an extract from a minute recording a resolution adopted unanimously at a meeting of the Council of this Society on the 23rd inst., as follows:

(1) *Conscious* of the responsibility solemnly laid upon us by the terms of our Charter of Incorporation, including and especially the responsibility to undertake and promote works for the extension of scientific knowledge
(2) *Noting* with concern the collective opinion of distinguished scholars members of our Society and of other scholars members of corresponding Societies *inter alia* the Russian State Academy of Physical and Biological Science and the North American Joint Institute for Environmental Research on the depletion of the ozone layer and of the polar ice masses, the accelerating warming of water masses, the progressive decline in fertility of agricultural areas heretofore producing the bulk of the food grains supporting rapidly expanding populations in China, western Russia, Europe, Africa, India, and North and South America, the defoliation of oxygenating arboreal climax forest in India, South America, and southeast Asia
(3) *Deploring* the consequent periodic occurrences of famine and widespread starvation suffered by many millions of persons throughout the world
(4) *Desiring* to assist in the alleviation of the hardship attendant upon the conditions above adumbrated
(5) *Conscious also* of the meritorious services rendered by William Bligh, Lieutenant, Astronautical Fleet, when serving

under the late lamented Captain James Cook, A.F., and the skill and daring with which he the said Bligh did successfully recover from Deep Space the Complex put at risk by the melancholy events surrounding the death of said Capt. Cook

(6) *Acknowledging* the value to science of the discovery of the fruit Tree reported in the zone denoted Titan 1014 during the course of the late lamented Capt. Cook's explorations

### THE COUNCIL OF THE SOCIETY HEREBY RESOLVES

1° To establish, equip, and supply an expedition to be known as the *Bounty of Nature Enterprise* for the exploration of remote asteroids, planets, and any and all such other heavenly bodies as that expedition may be able to visit and in particular of that zone denoted as Titan 1014 to the end that new sources of food for humankind may be identified, harvested, cloned, and adapted for use on Earth

2° To offer to William Bligh, Lieutenant, Astronautical Fleet, appointment as leader of said *Bounty of Nature Enterprise*

3° To invite said William Bligh to commence forthwith the recruitment and training of crew and laying-in of stores required for equipment and supply of said expedition

4° To recommend to the Supreme Command of the Astronautical Fleet that said William Bligh be promoted to the rank of Commander as from the date of his acceptance of the commission hereby entrusted to him

5° To solicit the cooperation of the United Nations Space Exploration Agency and of such other bodies as may be appropriate for the equipping, launching, monitoring, flight control, and return of the said *Bounty of Nature Enterprise.*

I am happy to inform you that the Supreme Command of the Astronautical Fleet has graciously signified its readiness to act upon the recommendation contained in par 4° above.

I have the honour to remain, Sir, your obedient and humble servant,

Elizabeth Richtungen
Secretary

Upon receipt of this communication, Lieut. Bligh, as he still was, repaired as soon as might be to the headquarters of the Astronautical Fleet, where, duly signifying his acceptance of the Royal Society's invitation, he was invested with the traditional crown and anchor of a Commander. He then proceeded to the seat of the Royal Society at Greenwich, alighting from the local rapid-transit train at Island Gardens, then going on foot through the old cast-iron tunnel under the Thames, emerging near that mysterious point bearing the ordinate 'zero' in the division of the rotundity of Earth's orb into degrees of longitude. Here he paused for a moment near the Cook Memorial to do homage to his late Commander, whose mastery of navigation and chronometry had enabled man for the first time to escape from the confines of serial time and space and to enter the pleated parameters of high velocities of mass and fractionalisations of time approaching infinity.

The *Bounty of Nature Enterprise* was already assembled in low Earth orbit and the officers of the Society and Commander Bligh quickly arranged with the appropriate agencies for the series of frequent shuttle flights needed to ferry supplies and equipment to the massive Complex.

Prospective crew members were empaneled, screened, trained, tested, screened again, and a final selection at last added to the *Bounty*'s articles. Bligh spoke no word in favour of a young kinsman of his mother, Fletcher Christian, who was among the orig-inal candidates and won through to the final list as Captain's Mate, but permitted himself a moment of satisfaction on learning of his young relative's success.

Aboard *Bounty,* each member of the crew, including the Captain, had an appointed bunk and workstation, amply fitted with combined restraints against both high G forces and weightlessness, and in these recesses, disposed in an array around the central chamber of the Complex, the crew spent their time monitoring on screens before them the digitised information streaming through on the performance of the craft—its condition, attitude, course, and speed, the state of its supplies of nutrients and other necessary materials, configuration of gravitational fields of heavenly bodies flanking its track, meteorite showers, detected and logged down to microparticle mass—all in accordance with a flight plan elaborated by Commander Bligh in close collaboration with the scientists appointed by the Society to oversee the general management of the expedition.

The central chamber of the Complex was a large hollow cylinder, dedicated to more social aspects of the crew's existence, be it face-to-face communication with one another or with the Captain (other communication being facilitated person-to-person, by closed voice-lines from each station to each of the others). In the central chamber, too, known by ancient tradition as the 'mess deck,' was equipment for the prescribed and voluntary physical exercises which the crew undertook to maintain body weight, muscle tone, tissue condition, bone strength, capacity and pressure of heart, lungs, and other organs. And the mess deck, as its name implies, was as well the place where the crew met for communal meals, each member seat-belted to the appointed place and quickly accustomed to feeding, almost like a baby, from the nozzles of supply tubes.

Last visits made to Earth base, last ferry trips completed, the *Bounty* cruised easily in low orbit as the hour of departure ticked closer. 'Adams, take your first fix.' 'First fix taken, sir, Archangel's beam right on the button.' 'Thank you, Adams, please confine yourself to approved terminology, prepare for second fix.' 'Second fix taken, sir, Starbuck Island dead ahead.' 'Thank you, prepare for third fix.' 'Third fix taken, sir, Mount Gabriel's beam dead ahead.' As these last terrestrial markers flipped past, Bligh, on the edge of Near Space, bethought him of his youthful cruises to remote waters in traditional sailing craft, round the southern tip of Ireland, calling to the tiny sporting harbour of Skull, beneath Mount Gabriel with its summit crowned by twin spheres of navigation aids, of a journey into grey Arctic seas, briefly in summer free of ice, of musky Pacific islands near the Line, each orbital pass a rhumb line connecting these remote places. With no time for reverie, he called: 'Mr. Kane, prepare propulsion.' 'Propulsion prepared, sir,' replied the engineer. 'Await ground signal, Mr. Kane.' 'Standing by for ground signal, sir.'

The last crackling voice signal came from Earth Control. 'Propulsion on zero, *Bounty,* and good luck. Ten, nine, eight . . .' At 'zero' Kane touched a cell on his display and each of the crew members experienced a sudden if brief black-out. After an interval—how long, how short, they knew not—clarity was restored and Bligh called out commands, so often rehearsed. 'Retract aerials and aerofoils.' 'Aerials retracted, sir.' 'Aerofoils retracted, sir,' and the *Bounty of Nature Enterprise* sped silently on into the blackness of Deep Space.

At a fixed time each morning, if one dare call them so, Bligh gave the command 'Mr. Christian, prepare D. med-scan' (that is, prepare to perform the daily medical examination of the members of the crew), whereupon Christian, touching the appropriate cell on his display (commonly called the 'dash' among cosmonauts), connected a sensitive apparatus to those terminals already attached to parts of the bodies of members of the crew, as skin (to detect temperature, moisture, salinity), wrist and chest (to measure heartbeat and pressure of the blood), certain subcutaneous implantations (to determine toxicity of the blood and its constituents), and so forth. On Christian's calling 'D. med-scan prepared, sir,' Bligh gave the further order 'Execute D. med-scan,' and Christian, touching the 'run' cell on his dash, implemented the procedures already so carefully prepared.

Within some seconds of the execution of the order, lights signifying the reported condition of each member of the crew would flash on Christian's display, a green light signifying healthy condition or condition within normal parameters, a red light signifying a reading without these tolerances. If no anomaly showed, Christian reported 'Instruments in green, sir,' and the procedure was deemed complete.

Each morning, as we have called them, at '0800 TET' (eight o'clock, terrestrial elapsed time, in the jargon of the cosmonauts), Bligh and Christian carried out this routine and we may judge of their surprise when one morning in midcourse, Christian, following an unwonted pause, reported 'Red on no. 3, sir.' Bligh gave the order 'Reprise D. med-scan,' and the operation was carried out again from beginning to end with the same disquieting outcome. Bligh then instructed Christian to isolate terminal 3 and to institute more searching examination, as a result of which the Captain determined that the crew member designated no. 3 (Dr. Metcalfe) was recording a deficiency in the functioning of her autoimmune system. Followed a private conversation between the Captain and Dr. Metcalfe touching intimate aspects of the private life of the latter and in particular her perceived failure to report in full to Astronautical Command the totality of her physiological history and condition as required at the rigorous examination carried out on her recruitment.

Bligh had then to reflect solemnly upon the outcome of this discussion. He knew beyond reasonable doubt that a member of his crew was suffering from an irreversible morbid condition and that her condition was such as to render her not merely a liability to the

Enterprise but a positive danger to her comrades and to the native peoples of the planets to which the Enterprise was directed. Here then was a classical ethical dilemma and one which devolved upon a commander the exercise of the most awesome responsibilities in him vested, and it was with a heavy heart that he later opened the channel which gave protected communication between himself and his medical officer. She, though stricken with grief, guilt, and fear, acknowledged her error and loyally allowed her fate to be at the sole disposition of her Captain, who instructed her to administer to herself a lethal injection, which, without a word of farewell to comrades, she silently and immediately did.

It had not escaped Bligh that he was faced with the problem of disposing of the body of his late medical officer, now lying in her combined bunk and workstation subject to the biological changes due to human remains in the environment, artificially maintained though it be, of normal atmosphere at normal ambient temperature. After some cogitation, he addressed his subordinate through closed-circuit communication, instructing him to verify remaining levels of uranium core. Came a reply from Christian, indicating a wish for confirmation of a command misunderstood or wrongly heard. 'Please say again, sir, I read "confirm levels of uranium core," please confirm, sir.' 'You read correctly, Mr. Christian, you read correctly, please execute immediately.' 'Aye, aye, sir.'

Bligh called onto his dash the charts of those parts of the galaxy lying closest to *Bounty*'s track and made his decision. Again calling his subordinate on closed-circuit, he instructed Christian to prepare for selective propulsion changes. The response to his instruction being again a question—'Propulsion, sir? But we are in midcourse'—he spoke testily: 'Pray do not question my commands, Christian, execute immediately.' Christian forthwith complied, as did Mr. Kane, the engineer, following the series of commands which initiated an adjustment and brief ignition of the motors. Well aware that a body separated from his craft in normal interstellar flight would merely continue to accompany that craft as a neighbour, sharing its trajectory, Bligh had ordered a propulsion which now had *Bounty* moving toward the gravitational field of an unexplored star. The Captain opened his general communication channel to all his crew and gave them, in suitably grave tones, information of the loss they had sustained through the sudden and unexplained death of their comrade the medical officer. He advised further that her remains were to be disposed of, in accordance with Royal Society routine orders, in a ceremony continuing an ancient tradition of the sea.

The body of Dr. Metcalfe, in its space suit, was taken to the bay dedicated to the launch and recovery of cosmonauts on extravehicular activity. As *Bounty* entered the gravitational field of Bligh's chosen star, he ordered the EVA bay opened and the remains gently propelled into the void, then ordered further alterations in propulsion which returned *Bounty* to its original course, while the shrouded corpse drifted slowly to an orbit round the star's nearest satellite, curving either to a fiery end as it burned up in the satellite's atmosphere or, if atmosphere there was none, to a crash to the ground with immense velocity, inevitably returning to the infinitesimal particles of dust from whence it came.

No further untoward incident befell the *Bounty* in the course of its voyage to the Society Cluster. Captain and crew were kept at readiness by a regime of duties and exercises, relieved by socialising on the mess deck. Monitoring rosters were regularly changed so that each member of the crew became familiar with the duties of all. Pre-ignition and pre-landing drills were repeated, shuttle bays and the EVA bay regularly cleared and tested. A humdrum existence, indeed, extending in elastic time until landfall at Titan (or Taheetan) was expected within the hour.

Monitor vigilance was placed on extra alert, ground sensors switched on. Eventually, in a series of routines now becoming familiar even to conservative earth-bound travelers, the *Bounty of Nature Enterprise* dipped into low orbit in Near Space and the first landing party boarded the shuttle to ferry down.

Bligh, Christian, and a few others landed amid scenes which were at once nostalgic and frightening for Bligh, merely wondrous for the others. The deepest forebodings felt by Bligh were set at rest and his function as diplomat and peacemaker little called upon when it became clear that the dreadful end of his late Commander Cook was deemed by the Taheetanians to have been a full, exact, and equalising sacrifice for the sacrilegious offence at the Tree and so to have left no residual ill-feeling.

With relief, then, Bligh, who had retained some mastery of the local language, could introduce his crew to their hosts, re-establish the old camp, and, with mixed distaste and resignation, contemplate the easy relations which quickly developed between the members of his crew and the beautiful, bare-chested, and compliant young men and women of Taheetan. Christian in particular, Bligh observed, formed a relationship with the daughter of the venerable King and it was as a result of Christian's influence in that quarter that the Enterprise was enabled to prosecute the principal object of its venture—the harvesting and cloning of elements from the heretofore forbidden Bread Tree.

On the unexpected death of the King and the revelation that his daughter and Heiress Apparent was
with child by Christian (and thus by local custom in
seclusion for many months), there devolved upon
Christian, as Regent, certain of the ceremonial rights
and duties appertaining to the hereditary kingship,
including, his Captain noted with satisfaction, that of
first-cropping of new buds on the Tree. Thus early in
the local spring it became possible to prepare tissue
samples of the mysterious and fruitful Tree for duplica-
tion in the biological laboratory built for and dedicated
to this purpose.

Cloning and the growth of new cultures, their swelling from the round diaphanous sections of filmy tissue
mounted on slides into biologically active fluffy patches
of new, thick, life-bearing breadlike protein, paralleled
the growth of Christian's child in the swelling womb of
his secluded partner. But her happy parturition pre-
ceded by only a few weeks the declaration by Bligh that
the cloning of the Tree had been successfully accomplished, and Christian's joy was immediately dashed
by the prospect of an imminent return to Earth.

Bligh could not permit what he considered mere
entanglements on the part of his crew to interfere with
the planned progress of his Enterprise and on the due
day gave orders for the initiation of loading and
launch-preparation procedures. Such orders, it is
hardly necessary to add in view of his circumstances,
were not welcome hearing for Christian, who hinted
to his superior that some other member of the well-
qualified crew might be entrusted with the tasks of
second-in-command while he might be released from
his articles to remain with his Royal Consort and their
child. This proposal found, as might be expected, little
favour with the Captain and it was with a heavy heart
that Christian bade an affectionate and tearful fare-

well to the Queen and their son as he joined the last
ferry party on the shuttle to join *Bounty,* finding there,
in an atmosphere once congenial, a sad contrast with
the free and open life, under sun and stars, in woods
and gardens, he had enjoyed, so briefly did it now seem,
with his royal and beautiful companion.

Bligh knew that he could expect some resentment
among a crew accustomed to that life of ease and free-
dom on their return to the artificial environment of the
*Enterprise* Complex, but assured himself that strict
adherence to routine orders and to the traditions of the
Fleet and its predecessors would soon re-establish his
vessel's complement as the well-drilled and contented
company of his outward voyage.

Shuttles stowed, aerials retracted, bay doors closed,
locked, and sealed—'the aircraft cleaned up,' as the old
pilots would have said—*Bounty* continued in low orbit
for a day of shakedown activities. Crew required re-
habituation to weightlessness, to being held in their
bunks and other stations with hook-tufted harnesses,
to nourishment from extruded foods and drinks. All
this was accomplished to the Commander's satisfaction
and he discreetly withdrew from the evening's socialising of his crew on the mess deck.

Next morning, Bligh himself activated the single-A
drive which carried the Complex tangentially to a
preplanned point on the edge of Deep Space where it
hung briefly counterpoised by the gravitational forces
of large though invisibly distant bodies. From his
command station, Bligh opened communication to all
crew members and was nonplussed on receiving no
confirmation of receipt of his order to Mr. Kane, the
engineer, to prepare nozzles on the Double-A drive for
ignition. Allowing a brief silence, Bligh called again:
'Mr. Kane, prepare nozzles alpha through delta for
ignition,' adding, in an unwonted gesture of levity,

'did the fellow smuggle some illicit drink on board last night?' He became alarmed when his command, even though couched in this light vein, still failed to elicit a response and he called to his immediate subordinate, 'Mr Christian, please confirm Kane is in a posture to receive commands.'

He scarce believed his ears when the monosyllabic reply came—'NO'—and fearing that his voice might break with the throat contraction of rising anger, he breathed deeply for a few seconds before responding. 'Mr. Christian, I hope I misheard. You will please confirm—' but at this juncture he heard, not a reply from Christian over the intercommunication network, but nearby the sound of tearing steps as someone approached his workstation with rapid strides along the hook-tufted trackway.

His own security straps were roughly torn from their fastenings as he struggled with Christian and two other assailants bursting into his workstation and, thus released, he shot clumsily onto the wider mess deck, there to swing helplessly through the air and bump against the far bulkhead. The others came rip-rippingly after and rapidly immobilised him, face to the bulkhead, with further strapping. 'It is no, Bligh, NO,' cried Christian, 'we will not prepare for blast-out, I will not force Kane to something so hateful.'

Consider the mountaineers who have climbed with the sure and swift foot of the chamois to the summit of Mont Blanc or the Matterhorn. They stand at the pinnacle, filled with the hubris of their achievement, when suddenly, mayhap, the noonday sun begins to melt the snow and ice on which they stand and all their earthly support begins to collapse beneath them. A quaking in the belly, an emptiness within, a dread tingling of the limbs, suddenly afflicts them. And it was thus with Bligh, faced with the awful prospect of mutiny by his crew on the remote edge of Deep Space. 'Is this mutiny, Mr. Christian?' he managed to ask. 'Your command has been incompetent, we are taking this vessel.' 'Just three of you?' asked Bligh, regaining some composure. 'The rest will follow, and if they don't they'll go where you're going.'

These were ominous words indeed and Bligh felt a tightening of the heart as his captors bundled him toward an exit bay, soon to be followed there by a few others, roughly pinioned. The captives were hustled swiftly into the shuttle dock and there into the no. 1 shuttle (the nearest to the docking arm) and told in uncouth terms that their fate was in their own hands. Sealing procedures were correctly followed when the captors withdrew, bay doors opened and the shuttle ejected slowly on its arm, dislodged under impulsion and hung poised near its parent craft. Regaining further composure, Bligh took the shuttle's command seat and deployed its antenna. '*Bounty,* Christian, do you read me? Do you read?' Silence. 'I abjure you, Christian, return to your duty.' Silence. The two craft still hung within televisual range but the *Bounty* with a sudden burst of ignition flashed into the distance, fading from the screen on Bligh's dash. In fury and some despair Bligh called a final threat that Christian and his fellow mutineers would yet face implacable justice and the final retribution of Execution Dock.

Bligh realised full well the dire situation in which he and his few loyal companions now found themselves. They were marooned in their tiny craft, with little sustenance for its systems or its human cargo or for its woefully weak motors. His frightened fellows stared at him in growing alarm and he drew no solace from their obvious dependance on him.

What a disastrous change in his circumstances! An hour since he commanded a sleek and polished sphere, supplied, equipped, and crewed for safe and fruitful journeys to remote Deep Space and back to Earth. Now his command had shrunk to a small and stubby shuttle, with low-grade aerodynamics, of perhaps some use in Near Space, of none at all in the deeper reaches. It was equipped with no more than the emergency supplies which might be needed during some brief mishap on short ferry journeys from ground to low orbit and it was crewed by a captain reduced in status and a few frightened ratings.

Bligh glanced about at his companions, saw them hanging awry from their harnesses, and realised the extreme loneliness of command. 'Very well, gentlemen,' he said (for all were men), 'let us relax a little and breathe quietly and regularly for a while as we consider our serious situation. And please smarten up a little, sloppiness will do us no good at all.' He spoke solemnly but with no panic in his voice. Grateful that their Captain spoke as one in control, they relaxed as bidden and for a few ensuing minutes Bligh pondered silently.

He recollected Cook's dictum—spaceships are not driven, they sail. He knew that he had little power for the initial impulsion of his craft and must plan its use with deadly precision and that an abyss of emptiness stretched between his craft and distant Earth; but he realised too that flanking any path it might follow were distant masses, invisible and vast, spreading gravitational fields through all Deep Space, waiting to push and pull his tiny ship on its way if only he could harness their forces. He remembered childhood games. Once, as a boy, he had set up a random array of magnets on a sloping board and laughed as a metal ball bearing staggered back and forth as it tried to roll down the board between them. He remembered arcade games of his youth, a heavier metal ball bounced hither and thither by the coiled springs around successive obstacles to its path through a maze.

Still in the pilot's station, he activated the shuttle's command dash and confirmed that the full range of astro-charts, though seldom consulted on the shuttle's normal journeys, was stored in its memory bank. 'Very well, gentlemen,' he said again, 'we are in a fairly desperate situation but on consideration I am confident that we have sufficient resources available to make a safe return to Earth. It will require careful planning and the most severe sacrifices but is, I repeat, within our capabilities.'

It proved to be the most difficult task of his career—the plotting of a track, spiral or helical, curving or rushing straight, or twisting and turning through Deep Space, now recoiling from one great stellar mass or skimming off its field, now whirling and accelerating toward another, until the counterforce of yet another pulled the shuttle into roll or spin, pitch or yaw, ever onward on its homeward course. In terrestrial elapsed time the journey would take many months and Bligh put the crude facts of the case brutally before the loyal but frightened men sharing his cramped space and his risks. 'We have power and supplies,' he explained, 'easily to accomplish a journey back to Titan, there to place ourselves at the mercy of the bloodthirsty mutineers who have, in all probability, already landed there. Or with careful husbanding of our material we can, as I have already suggested, most probably effect a successful return to Earth. Before nozzle preparation and power ignition I must have your assent to my undertaking one or another of these journeys.'

The confidence of his hearers in his ability to bring them safely home restored to Bligh a measure of confidence in himself, sadly deflated by his encounter with Christian and the mutineers. 'I thank you, gentlemen,' he replied to their muttered chorus of approval, 'but I must warn you that the meagre snack lunches for ferry trips with which this little craft is victualed will be severely rationed to sustain us over the months of our voyaging.'

Meticulous study of the astro-charts, repeated drills in launch procedures, checking and rechecking, again and again, of the nozzles and core resources, were followed eventually by that dread moment when Bligh, his voice now calm, called: 'Co-pilot, this is not a drill, repeat, this is not a drill, we are entering an executive sequence, we are entering an executive sequence. Please respond and confirm understanding.' 'Understood, sir, this is not a drill, we are entering executive sequence.' 'Prepare nozzles beta through gamma for ignition.' 'Nozzles beta through gamma prepared, sir.' 'On zero, ignite nozzles beta through gamma.' 'On zero, will ignite nozzles beta through gamma.' 'Ten, nine, eight . . .' On 'zero' a loin-shuddering tremor rocked the frail vessel but shortly after, on the easing of strain on their harnesses, all were reassured when Bligh gave another and quieter command. 'All crew at ease on low alert. And thank you.'

The hazardous journey had not long begun when Bligh realised that he must supplement the exiguous tube rations on which the shuttle's team were subsisting if they were to survive through the millions upon millions of kilometres which stretched before them. He opened a sealed vacuum canister, stowed in a recess in the hull of the shuttle for earliest delivery to Earth on the planned Earth-fall, now, like so much of the rest of his planning, totally abandoned and in disarray. It contained the precious cloned specimens of the tissues taken from the once-forbidden Tree. He carefully counted the small round wafers of breadlike nutrient; each would provide a mouthful. Hesitantly, but with a

secret hope, he broke the bread and offered a portion
to each of his companions, then consumed a portion
himself. It tasted good and gave more than expected
satisfaction. Next day, as the tube rations squeezed
nearer to exhaustion, he reopened the canister and was
exhilarated to note that the ambient atmosphere had
reenergized the broken wafers and each had regrown
almost to its original size. Reassured now, as well as
reinvigorated, the space waifs could contemplate with
more equanimity the prospect of their remaining jour-
neying and the perils of landing.

As the *Bounty*'s shuttle reentered the solar system,
Bligh, in some trepidation, gave the order 'Deploy solar
panels' and was relieved when the response 'Solar
panels deployed, sir' confirmed that that part at least
of his equipment had survived the rigours of the immense voyage. As they sailed closer to the sun, positive
charging by the panels was recorded and Bligh ordered
'Deploy aerials.' On receipt of 'Aerials deployed, sir,'
he opened the channel for voice communication and
sent a distress call to all stations which might hear
it. '*Bounty* shuttle 1 to Enterprise Mission Control.
We want permission to land. This is *Bounty* shuttle 1,
repeat *Bounty* shuttle 1, seeking permission to land.'
After a moment's silence—shocked silence, Bligh imagined—on the part of the controller on Earth, a thin and
scratchy but reassuring voice replied 'Enterprise Mission Control to *Bounty,* say again please, I read *Bounty*
shuttle seeking permission to land.' '*Bounty* shuttle,
repeat shuttle, to Mission Control. I confirm shuttle
seeks permission to land.' 'I read you, *Bounty* shuttle,
permission granted, will advise—but how come you
didn't call from *Bounty?*'

But that was a long story which would have to wait,
as Bligh, in communication with ground control, tested
gently the rough and heavy aerodynamic controls of

the shuttle, then took it into a series of gradually tight-ening orbits which slowed it at the cost of heating it near to the limits of tolerance. Slipping incandescent through the stratosphere, the shuttle finally went into a long shallow glide and scraped its way to a safe land-ing at the extreme limit of a salt-pan runway in the southwest of the United States.

Of the extensive notice in the press covering the unexpected return to Earth of the shuttle without its mother ship it is unnecessary to repeat details here. Nor is it necessary to give the lie to the many false and malicious rumours circulated in the press and in unworthy pamphlets by Grub Street hacks touching the unhappy events on the *Bounty*'s voyage. Suffice to say that the Court of Enquiry appointed by the Royal Society to try into the matter of the loss of his com-mand, the *Bounty of Nature Enterprise,* by Commander William Bligh, and the death of his medical officer Dr. Metcalfe, found William Bligh entirely blameless and he has thereafter continued his illustrious career with-out a stain upon his character.

# An Appendix
## to the
## Narrative &c., &c.

S tartling new intelligence bearing on the fate of the
miscreants who revolted against their lawful master in taking mutinous possession of the *Bounty of
Nature Enterprise* has come to the scientific community with the return to Earth after a long voyage of
the hunting vessel *Charles W. Morgan,* of New Bedford,
Mass., and the relation of her master, Mr. Israel
Hands, of that vessel's proceedings in a little-charted
zone of the galaxy while about its legitimate business
of hunting for protein fauna.

Mr. Hands presents himself as a plain and simple
man but has felt compelled to indict a more detailed
narrative of part of his cruise than would be contained
in the brief daily log which is all he is required by law
to maintain. He has kindly placed his remarkable narrative in the hands of the redactor of these pages who
draws upon it freely in his presentation of the following
account.

'I am a plain and simple man,' he writes, 'and master
of a plain and simple craft. We have communications
enough, as required by law, for our direction-finding in
Near Space. Nobody has ever dared say Israel Hands
has caused a mishap on launch or landfall. We don't
have fancy channels for remote voice-contact and so
my story, and it is a very perplexing story, has had to
wait for my return home. Of course we're a hunting
ship and we have sensors to tell us if there's life below

us as we cruise through the galaxy.'

As they approached a sector denominated LS/2/47/
06, Mr. Hands records, his hunting officer reported
signals of biological activity on the largest of a group
of satellites orbiting a binary white dwarf. Closer cruising and rescanning confirmed the signals and Mr.
Hands and a small party embarked on their simple
shuttle to effect a landing in the area identified as
source of the strongest signal.

On landing and emerging from their shuttle, they
were astonished to find themselves surrounded by an
excited group of men and women speaking English
and garbed in the fashion of an earlier age. 'Plain man
though I be,' writes Mr. Hands, 'I go to church when
at home and know well from Rev. Eliot that there are
principalities and powers beyond our understanding.'
He feared, in fact, that these people were but phantoms
in minds troubled by the loneliness of Deep Space and
cast a glance back and forth among his comrades. All,
however, seemed convinced, as he was, that, beyond
belief as it might seem, the people of this small planet
were people indeed, as human as those walking Johnny
Cake Hill in New Bedford.

They were a handsome people, these Planeteers,
black of hair and bronze of skin, and kindly too, and
made their visitors welcome with the courtesies of
society; they gave food and drink, goat's flesh and
juices of sweet fruits, and bade their guests come with
them to the town, which proved to be a short street of
houses built in the most simple manner, with corner-
posts fashioned from tree-trunks and walls and roofs
of plaited grass. Though shy, the Planeteers were soon
plying their visitors with questions: who were they?
whence came they? why did they come? what message
did they bring? was it one to inspire hope or fear? The
visitors, in their turn, had as many questions to ask,

many of them of the same form: who were these people? whence came they? who were their ancestors?

'Often had I heard' (we quote Mr. Hands again) 'strange tales of old voyagers from the New England coast who had blasted off from bases in Florida and California, aye and Central Asia, never to return. Had some of them landed in this remote spot?'

To the question 'what is the name of this place?' there came the reply which further deepened the suspicions of Mr. Hands. 'Why, this be the Pit,' the Planeteers told him, and in further replies told that they were all descended from Adams. This caused Mr. Hands to give thanks to God and to his pastor the Rev. Eliot for the grace which led him to understand that he and his crew and these Planeteers were indeed brothers and sisters, but he was completely taken aback by the remark next volunteered by one of their hosts: 'There be many tales of the old times, but you must ask Mr. Adams himself, he'll tell you all.'

'Pious and God-fearing people we may be,' wrote Hands, 'but we are plainspoken Yankees, and no hayseeds from remote parts can put one across us. This was plain flap-doodle.' Pained by the visitors' disbelief, the Planeteers pressed their views and insisted that Mr. Hands seek confirmation of what they said from 'old Mr. Adams.'

Could this be, wondered Mr. Hands, no more than a monstrous coincidence? There were folk named Adams throughout Massachusetts, two of them had been early presidents of the United States; indeed, kin of his own had married into a family of the name in Fall River, an old town, once a settlement of the Pilgrim Fathers, not far from his home in New Bedford, and there were others of the name in Milton, not much farther away, though they were farming folk and not voyagers.

Hands and his fellow visitors made their way, as urged, to the house pointed out as the home of 'old Mr. Adams' and there to their continuing wonderment were received by a venerable gentleman whose wrinkled and sunken cheeks, frail limbs, and long white hair and beard betokened an age belied in part by a piercing glance from the glittering eyes. 'I bid ye welcome, whoever ye be,' said Mr. Adams, 'pray tell me how came ye to these parts?'

Hands explained that they were hunting for protein-bearing fauna, there being a ready market for such among the teeming population of Earth, increasingly suffering from malnutrition as the meagre resources of that planet came closer and closer to exhaustion. 'Aye, could be, could be,' responded Adams, 'but there's little in your line here. You've no other reason for visiting us? You're not, perchance, to look for me?' 'Sir,' said Hands, 'though you are clearly the leader of a happy community, I pledge my honour I had never heard of "the Pit," as your people tell me this place is called, until they told me of it on our landing from our shuttle and if I mistake not, and I am a traveled man, there is no other man on Earth has heard of it besides. Who would send me hither?' 'Bligh, mayhap? The Society?' queried the old man; then Hands to him replying: 'I know no Bligh, nor do I know any society of which you may be speaking. I am a lone hunter.' 'Maybe so, maybe so, Mr. Hands. Anyway, we be peaceful and kindly people and will treat you well the while you are amongst us.'

Much of Mr. Hands's account, as will have been clear even from the foregoing, is couched in the form of reported statements, the reported statements often in their turn reporting further statements; as, for example, 'Mr. Adams told me that Christian had told him that Bligh had said . . .' To avoid the encumbrances of such *oratio obliqua* we have given ourselves the editorial liberty to translate the whole into *oratio recta* and as Mr. Adams was Mr. Hands's sole informant no risk of confusion need arise and truth, verisimilitude, and clarity will be at once the better served.

Know, then, that *Bounty* spent one year at Titan, as the local inhabitants had learnt from their visitors to call it but which became in their speech Taheetan. The main complex of *Bounty* remained in medium-level orbit, untended save for the presence on board of Mr. Adams as ship-keeper. Bligh and the rest of the crew established a camp on the surface and prepared for the one-year stay, that length of sojourn being determined by the necessity to secure, prepare, and prove tissue sections for cloning of the Bread Tree, yielding fruit after her kind. 'It was that forbidden Fruit Tree,' said Adams, 'whose mortal taste brought death into the world, and all our woes.'

Bligh himself, as a result of the death on the outward journey of the medical officer, Dr. Metcalfe, was the person responsible for the scientific work of the expedition, the rest of the crew being but lightly occupied in the minor tasks of camp maintenance. In enforced near-idleness, these young men and women quickly fell into self-indulgent ways and entered into deep and intimate relations with the healthy, beautiful, and compliant young men and women of the locality. To these young natives such relationships were as natural as the breathing of the balmy air of their earthly paradise, the drinking of the sparkling waters of their pure streams, or the feasting on the abundant fruits of their exuberant woods and gardens.

Bligh, at first outraged by the hedonistic behaviour of his crew but later resigned to it, noted in particular, with a cynical and exploitative eye, the regular cohabitation of his assistant Christian with the daughter of the austere and aloof King of the community. He slyly encouraged the younger man in his *amour,* seeming in conversation to condemn lechery but with shrug and wink confessing to an older man's inability to control the hot blood of youth.

The village soon rejoiced at the news of the young Princess's pregnancy and with gay laughter decked her and the father of her child-to-be with wreaths of choice blooms from the forest. The feasting lasted day after day and reached its climax at a great banquet celebrating the conception of an heir or heiress to the throne and attended by the King himself. Little did his happy majesty suspect what evil was privily contrived by his principal guest at the feast, the lord and master of the father of his newly conceived grandchild. Never plotting evil nor fearing any, the King took the gourd of heady liquor proffered by Capt. Bligh toward the close of the festivities. Soon after, he excused himself from further entertainment of his guests and retired to his home. There his pregnant daughter found him dead the next morning.

The people of Taheetan were used to death, which occurred only when men and women had reached great age and serenity, then fading, as it were, back into the ground whence all things grew. The late King, though old, had not yet reached the usual age of quiet dissolution and his death caused some dismay. Grief, anguish, distress, were unknown to the people of Taheetan. He was, however, of such maturity and had had such a full and complete life that his obsequies were performed quickly and happily and eyes were turned expectantly on the young visitor Christian, consort of the late King's heiress.

'Don't you understand, Christian,' asked Bligh, 'what happens here when a woman is with child? When she misses her first monthly period we have rejoicings such as we have seen in the case of your young woman.' Christian bridled at the use of such abrupt language to describe his charming partner and remonstrated with his superior. 'As you like, Christian, as you like. Remember I have the powers of a commander and will marry you tomorrow in good old English fashion if that's your wish. But do it quickly. Before her next monthly period would have been due she must retire into seclusion, and be tended only by women beyond childbearing age. And you, Christian, will act as King until she comes to term.'

The status of Regent, which devolved upon the young officer in this unexpected fashion, entailed little performance of duties other than ceremonial functions, in such a peaceful, self-sufficient, and self-regulating community and Christian, now separated from his Queen, continued to be busy about the maintenance duties of the *Bounty* Enterprise and lived again in the encampment erected by the *Bounty*'s people in the area devoted by their hosts to the purposes of their visitors.

There Christian was surprised one morning by his captain, addressing him in familiar terms. 'Good morrow, King Christian, the spring weather is charming, is it not?' 'I beg your pardon, sir,' replied Christian, as stiffly as he thought fitting in one of lower rank speaking to a superior. 'Springtime, man, springtime, you've had your fill of the birds and the bees, the trees are in bud, or haven't you noticed?' 'Indeed they are so, sir, is it not in the way of nature?' Bligh then reminded him of the high purpose of their mission, thus explaining his reference to nature and the budding of the trees, and continued: 'It's time now for us to take our specimens and set about our scientific work. You do realise, I take it, that you are empowered by the ancient tradition of these people to be the one who will cut the first fruiting buds from the Bread Tree?'

Whereupon a dark cloud of suspicion descended on the mind of Christian, suspicion that his love and his fatherhood, the death of the King, the seclusion of his spouse (clearly foreknown to Bligh), were parts of a deep and evil plot hatched by the Captain in his monomaniac attachment to the scientific objectives of the Enterprise. Christian was loth to give offence but reluctant to commit himself to the exercise of a prerogative for which he felt his title was at least doubtful, and he expressed a mild demurrer, whereat Bligh exploded in wrath: 'I call you to your duty, sir. I am your commanding officer, we have a task imposed on us, let us set about it. A year's enough for our purposes, already we have hung about here idle for three months, we have built a biological lab, and still haven't got one slide of tissue to work on. I know what you're thinking, mistake me not. Nine months is enough for any wench to come to term, you'll see your brat before we leave!'

Christian bridled again at the dismissive words used by his captain about the gentle mother of his child-to-be and, full of hesitation, made bold to reply. 'She is my wife, sir, in the eyes of God and man, married to me by yourself, sir, in accordance with the laws of England. You would oblige me by not speaking of her in such terms. And as to the child, I had hoped—' 'You had hoped, you dolt, that I would permit you to break the terms of your articles and stay in this paradise of luxury and idleness; but never, sir, never, we have a duty to do, get you to it.' And Bligh turned on his heel and walked away.

The beauty of the forest about him as he slowly climbed the stout bole of the once-forbidden Tree was in sad contrast to the heaviness of the young man's heart. The foliage of last year was awaiting the bursting forth of the new; stray old leaves adhered, adorned with the silver cocoons of busy insects spinning their silky filaments, here and there a last year's bloom remained, still bravely showing its gay yellow in the shade of an old leaf, a few thick nuts, unharvested, still hung, and at the growing tip the tender shoots of new branch stems were breaking forth in light green from lipped orifices in the axils of the old. Almost feeling a pain he imagined in his victim, Christian sliced off sections from the tiny green cones and bestowed them in their prepared canister, sealed and exhausted it to sustain their original atmospheric environment, and as slowly descended from his lofty pinnacle.

Christian was not the only one of the *Bounty*'s people involved with a Titanian lover but his affair with the Princess, now Queen, overshadowed all the others in importance. The attention which it caused to be given to him made Christian more resentful than any of the others of Bligh's insistence on a prompt and early departure for Earth as soon as the biogenetic work on the Tree tissues had been successfully completed. Christian's bitterness was gradually if perhaps unintentionally spread by a word here, a sour look there, a shrug of sulkiness or mock resignation. The routine of their ordered life kept all crew members outwardly conforming to correct discipline and it was only the anguish of parting from his Queen that finally swept Christian to the denunciations he uttered to his fellows when Bligh circumspectly left them alone on that first evening in midlaunch, as *Bounty* hung poised and counterpoised on the edge of Deep Space.

It was here that Christian expressed openly for the first time the fear and suspicion seething within him ever since Bligh had bluntly forced him to desecrate the Tree so sacred to Taheetan, suspicion that Bligh was somehow implicated in the death of the King and fear of the consequences of giving utterance to that suspicion. A half-spoken word from him was enough to unleash a flood of recrimination from his fellows. One complained of the Captain's refusal to ship some supplies of fresh food from Taheetan for the return journey, another of his refusal to extend their stay for further and more thorough proving of the cloned Tree tissues, a third of the enforced and unnecessary doubling of ship-keeping rosters during the latter days of launch preparation, yet another complained of an unjustified confining of the company to their small encampment during the same period. And another darkened the atmosphere even more by asking the barbed question: And what had happened to Dr. Metcalfe anyway?

So there were no eve-of-launch jokes and laughter that evening, no lottery on estimated time of arrival, no coarse jests, even, at the expense of romantic partners they were leaving behind. Instead a mood of sullen nastiness, which took focus at last among a small group when the rest had retired to their bunks. A group who in a few quick whispered sentences gave shape and form to their pent-up resentments and plotted the events of the morrow: the refusal to obey orders, the wresting of control of the Complex from Bligh, and a speedy return to Taheetan.

The simple plan was easily put into operation. When Bligh paused for a few seconds, as the plotters knew he must on their refusal to obey an order, Christian and his closest associates swiftly made their way to his workstation and rendered him powerless. As swiftly, they canvassed those not privy to their plan: Are you for us or against us? Those declaring themselves 'against' were bundled with Bligh to the shuttle bay, where Bligh, expostulating, made an appeal to Christian in the name of the scientific objective of their Enterprise.

Christian, in a passion, rushed to the storage bays of the Complex and tore from their holdfasts the canisters of cloned Tree tissue; thrusting these at Bligh, he burst out: 'Take your lousy specimens, and may they rot in space with you and the rest of your stinking traitors!'

Having cast off the shuttle, Christian immediately assumed command and called out orders. His companions obeyed but with some show of reluctance; happy though they were to see the end of Bligh, they were unsure of the authority now being assumed by the former second-in-command. 'Kane, prepare for propulsion. Prepare to adjust throat attitude. Prepare nozzles for ignition. Quickly, man, quickly, confirm receipt and compliance.' The 'Aye, aye, sir' came, but slowly.

While these preparations were under way, the frail shuttle with its miserable complement was still within local communication range. Bligh was calling: 'Shuttle to *Bounty*, shuttle to *Bounty*, permit me to redock. Return to your duty and some accommodation can be arranged. Shuttle to *Bounty*, do you read?' As the greater craft shuddered with the ignition of its motor's emissions, the last cry the mutineers heard was in a different voice, a voice of towering rage from Bligh: 'Christian, you mutinous swine, I'll live to see you hanging from a gibbet!'

Plotting a reciprocal course, *Bounty* expended valuable motive core on a manoeuvre to reverse the craft and travel once more in the direction of Taheetan. On reaching this objective, Christian, who had by now assumed all the functions of a commander, ordered *Bounty* placed in low Near Space orbit. Adams was given his usual role of ship-keeper and Kane, piloting the smaller and only remaining shuttle, took a small party, of course including Christian, to a safe landfall. Needless to dwell upon the reunion of Christian and his Princess, though so to dwell might delay contemplation of sadder events then, perhaps mercifully, hidden in the future. 'As to what reasons Christian gave to his wife and his friends on Taheetan for the return there without Bligh,' Mr. Hands writes, 'Mr. Adams professed to have no knowledge at all.'

After the heady experiences of the previous few days, Christian was in an exalted frame of mind but soon came to a practical appraisal of his dire circumstances. He was, he knew, an outlaw, game to be hunted anywhere in the galaxies by agents of the Astronautical Fleet, and facing, if captured by them, nothing less than Execution Dock.

In blood still hot, then, he quickly determined his course, his self-esteem still falsely inflated by his brief experience as a Regent and an usurping commander. The Queen and the child were to join *Bounty* for a voyage to a new and secret destination. Strong young men and women of Taheetan were invited to accompany them. But who can regard an invitation from a Queen and her consort as less than a command?

The Queen and these Taheetan volunteers, having no training, were confused and made ill by the fierce rush of the shuttle to its docking orbit with the *Bounty* Complex, were frightened at being strapped into unfamiliar supernumerary bunks, and finally lost consciousness as the orders for propulsion adjustment and ignition echoed into their ears through the communication system. Later, drifting crazily about the mess deck, they were ordered to fasten themselves to sprung harness, invited to dine off extruded pastes, and to exercise their limbs thus and thus. . . . Silently they lamented their lost sparkling streams, fruitful gardens, clear skies, their happy community of kindly neighbours, their prattling children, their elders, quiet and meditative. Now all was command, do this, do that, prepare for this, prepare for that, all leading to an unknown destination in an unknown future.

'And it was dirty, I mean really dirty' (in Adams's words as reported by Hands verbatim), 'these people had no idea of weightlessness or G forces or high-velocity flight and they just threw up and in weightlessness can you imagine the filthiness of that mess deck? And these poor souls were so used to being clean, they were used to spending half their lives splashing naked in a clear warm sea. What good was a wipe with an absorbent/evaporant tissue to them? And we were crowded; the waste bags were strapped in corners, but you bumped into them as you moved about. And there was no privacy, even for intimate relations. It didn't mean much to the Taheetan folk but even when we lived amongst them there had been some decency among the visitors but here it was all jumbled together and things began to get a little edgy, I can tell you, when a visitor and a Taheetan man might both want the same Taheetan girl. They looked more beautiful than ever floating in weightlessness, more beautiful even than in the waters of their lagoons.'

Christian tried his best to command but could not easily mix being a captain and a king. To the crew he was Captain, in sort, and they would obey an order about the affairs of the craft, but not as regards the social life of the mess deck. And to the Taheetanians he was their King, but did not look like a king, having to struggle to have his way with the crew, and his authority with the Taheetanians too began to weaken.

Eventually he found himself isolated and turned morose, talked wildly sometimes to Adams, sometimes to himself, mumbling slowly, sometimes shouting to everybody, his eyes wild. And he shouted or mumbled the same things over and over, so much so that all the people on board began to know them and his sayings can still be heard among the people of the Pit, chanted

like proverbs, or as one might learn passages from the
Good Book as a child and continue to quote them all
through life.*

---

*Mr Hands's mate, Mr. Davidson, a good old singer of chauntey and
spiritual songs and an avid collector of popular superstitions and
lore, has favoured the editor with a transcription of a number of
these chants, attributed by the common people of the Pit to their
ancestor Christian, and we give here a selection of them as proving,
we hope, of interest to the cultural anthropologist and the ethno-
musicologist, the latter of whom may apply to Mr. Davidson for
copies of his notations of the simple tunes to which he has heard the
words fitted. Mr. Davidson is of the opinion that the singers have
failed to understand much of the material handed on by word of
mouth and have thus introduced corruptions. We confine ourselves
here to giving the following extracts and leave scholarly disputa-
tion on such matters to the learned in their academies.

(i)
Before their eyes in sudden view appear
The secrets of the hoary Deep,
A dark illimitable ocean without bounds,
Without dimension, where length, breadth and height
And time and place are lost,
With thousand thousand stars that then appeared
Spangling the hemisphere.

(ii)
Fluttering his pennons vain plumb down he drops
Ten thousand fathoms deep, then with expanded wings
He steers his flight aloft on dusky air
That felt unusual weight, till on dry land
He lights.

(iii)
Who shall tempt with wandering feet
The dark unbottomed infinite Abyss
And through the palpable obscure find out
The uncouth way or spread in airy flight
Upborne with indefatigable wings
Over the vast abrupt ere he arrive
The happy Isle, where is a place
The seat of some new race called Man.

Incoherent Christian may have been betimes but he had known what he was about when he set the *Enterprise* upon that course she was now predestinatedly following and the craft finally came, after due lapse of time and distance, to a habitable planet circling a minor star at the remote edge of the cluster earlier named for the Society. There he ordered the *Enterprise* put into low Near Space orbit and instituted preparations for a landing.

It took many shuttle journeys to ferry from the *Bounty* to ground its augmented human complement and the supplies taken on at Taheetan. The men and women taken from there, in particular, felt some joy at their release from the weightless confines of the spacecraft and stood with the rest on the seashore of a small island, in a quiet ocean, on a planet they had learnt to call 'the Pit.'

As the ferry journeys continued, Adams, accustomed to ship-keeping, remonstrated with Christian. 'If I'm to stay aboard, Christian, I'll need some supplies kept here.' 'You won't, Adams; what's the point of ship-keeping when there's nowhere else to go? *Bounty* is finished.'

---

(iv)
In mutual league united once,
In thoughts and counsel, equal hope
And hazard in the glorious Enterprise
Now joined in misery in equal ruin
Into what Pit thou seest
From what height fallen.


(v)
The crystal wall of heaven opening wide
Rolled inward and a spacious gap disclosed
Into the wasteful Deep.
Headlong themselves they threw
Down from the verge of heaven; eternal wrath
Burnt after them to the bottomless Pit.

Boarding for what proved to be the last ferry down, Christian ordered Adams to join him and before quitting the Complex adjusted the setting of the controls so that their shuttle's landfall was followed by a circling blaze across the sky as the *Bounty* descended from low orbit and burnt itself into the detritus of a shooting star.

Christian took the most usable parts of the shuttle's hull and fashioned a house for himself and his Queen on the slope of a small hill overlooking the sea inlet near which the landfall had been made. Other couples paired off and did as well as they might in the same line with the remainder.

'Oh, 'twas bad' (again we use Adams's words as reported by Hands), "twas very bad. The Taheetan people wanted to be home but there was no way of going there and if they couldn't have their own home they wanted at least their own men and women and the Earth people took them, an Earthwoman grabbing a Taheetan man or an Earthman grabbing a Taheetan girl. Then they all fell to fighting with wicked knives they made of bits of the metal from the hull or even with knives they chipped out of sharp stones they found in the ground or with heavy clubs they made out of round-rolled stones they found on the seashore.'

In response to Mr. Hands's questions, Adams told something of his own story, though in veiled terms. 'Aye, I had many women, my own, other men's wives that lost their husbands in the fights, Taheetan girls that there was no man left for after the fights. And lots of children.'

Of Christian's fate he would say little. 'I do remember what must have been nearly the last thing he said to me: "It was all because of that accursed Tree," he said, "it was no Bread Tree, it was a foul cross between the poisonous upas tree of Java and the Yggdrasil of the Vikings, 'twas poison spreading everywhere.'" But he did point out the place where the unhappy Christian met his end. 'Yon cliff-top there behind the hill where it beetles over the sea, he'd go there sometimes and wave his fists at the sky as if he was calling *Bounty* back. But of course there was no use to that. So another day he'd fall to cursing about the flight and the Deep or the Pit, all those things he'd shouted about on the long voyage, that's why the people called this place "the Pit," and waving his arms as if they were wings instead of fists, and one day we noticed he never came back and when we went looking we found his body dashed to pieces there on the rocks below the cliff, but how he came there no one ever knew or will know.'

The Queen too died soon after, of more natural causes, and soon nobody but Adams was left of the *Bounty* people, and nobody at all of those taken from Taheetan; only the ancient patriarch and a brood of younger persons of tawny skin, between brown and black, between yellow and white, labouring with simple tools to win sustenance from a demanding soil, knowing nothing of their past but old stories of the blazing comet in the sky, the King and Queen descending, and old Mr. Adams the father of them all.

'Of the truth of this story,' Mr. Hands concludes, 'I warrant nothing, merely that that is as I heard it from the lips of old Mr. Adams and his people and I set it down here in my log lest I forget the strange details. And my mate Mr. Davidson affirms this by his signature beside mine.'

# About the Author

Alf Mac Lochlainn was born in Dublin in 1926, studied at University College, Dublin (M.A., 1948), and became a librarian, with internships at the Library of Congress and Simmons College in Boston. He has been Director of the National Library of Ireland and Librarian of University College, Galway, chairman of the James Joyce Institute of Ireland, and a trustee of the Chester Beatty Library. He was inaugural holder of the Visiting Chair of Irish Studies at Burns Library, Boston College, from 1991 to 1992.

He has written scripts for radio, television, and short films (he was a member of the board of the Irish Film Theatre) and published numerous essays in bibliography, film criticism, and social and intellectual history, as well as satirical verse published in limited editions. His first book, a surrealist novella entitled *Out of Focus,* was published by O'Brien Press (Dublin) in 1977, and by Dalkey Archive in 1985.

Now in retirement, he is an active member of the Labour Party and lives in Galway with his wife Fionnuala ni Riain. They have six children.

# DALKEY ARCHIVE PRESS

*"The program of the Dalkey Archive Press is a form of cultural heroism—to put books of authentic literary value into print and keep them in print."*—JAMES LAUGHLIN

Our current and forthcoming authors include:

GILBERT SORRENTINO • DJUNA BARNES • ROBERT COOVER • WILLIAM H. GASS
YVES NAVARRE • COLEMAN DOWELL • HARRY MATHEWS • RENÉ CREVEL
LOUIS ZUKOFSKY • LUISA VALENZUELA • OLIVE MOORE • EDWARD DAHLBERG
JACQUES ROUBAUD • FELIPE ALFAU • RAYMOND QUENEAU • DAVID MARKSON
CLAUDE OLLIER • JOSEPH MCELROY • ALEXANDER THEROUX • MURIEL CERF
JUAN GOYTISOLO • TIMOTHY D'ARCH SMITH • PAUL METCALF • MAURICE ROCHE
CHRISTINE BROOKE-ROSE • MARGUERITE YOUNG • JULIÁN RÍOS • RIKKI DUCORNET
ALAN ANSEN • HUGO CHARTERIS • NICHOLAS MOSLEY • RALPH CUSACK
SEVERO SARDUY • KENNETH TINDALL • MICHEL BUTOR • VIKTOR SHKLOVSKY
THOMAS MCGONIGLE • CLAUDE SIMON • DOUGLAS WOOLF • MARC CHOLODENKO
OSMAN LINS • ESTHER TUSQUETS • MICHAEL STEPHENS • CHANDLER BROSSARD
PAUL WEST • RONALD FIRBANK • EWA KURYLUK • CHANTAL CHAWAF
STANLEY CRAWFORD • CAROLE MASO • FORD MADOX FORD • GERT JONKE
PIERRE ALBERT-BIROT • FLANN O'BRIEN • ALF MAC LOCHLAINN • PIOTR SWECZ
LOUIS-FERDINAND CÉLINE • PATRICK GRAINVILLE • W. M. SPACKMAN
JULIETA CAMPOS • GERTRUDE STEIN • ARNO SCHMIDT • JEROME CHARYN
JOHN BARTH • ANNIE ERNAUX • JANICE GALLOWAY • JAMES MERRILL
KAREN ELIZABETH GORDON • FERNANDO DEL PASO • SUSAN DAITCH
ALDOUS HUXLEY • WILLIAM EASTLAKE • LAUREN FAIRBANKS
WILFRIDO D. NOLLEDO • EVELIN SULLIVAN • C. S. GISCOMBE

To receive our current catalog, write to:

**Dalkey Archive Press, Campus Box 4241, Normal, IL 61790-4241
phone: (309) 438-7555; fax: (309) 438-7422**